Elysa's Savior

Heroes of Wolf Creek

By

R. J. Stevens

Cover Art: SelfPubBookCovers.com/JohnBellArt_89393

ISBN: 9798856031491
Printed in America

Dedication

To all my readers.
Thank you for your support.

Prologue

Elysa Goines allowed tears to fall from her brown eyes as she lay on the mattress wondering how she could have been so stupid. Everyone from her brother to the man she secretly loved tried to warn her, but did she listen? No.

She was an adult at the ripe old age of twenty-six. Between her brother and her dad, she could defend herself well, unless someone drugged her, which was why she landed in this dungeon.

Closing her eyes, she allowed regret to pierce her heart again for letting her friend set her up on a blind date at the annual Christmas party hosted by the magazine she worked for. Although she felt a deep-down warning when she met the man, she immediately dismissed the feeling when he explained an article his agent insisted, he take on.

Intrigued by his stories of working overseas in exotic places, she readily agreed to assist him on the project. Her heart broke just a little when he told her of his capture and ultimate torture by a rebel group near the border of Afghanistan.

Why on earth did she ignore not only the warnings of everyone she loved, but her own internal sense of impending doom? That mistake just might be the last one she'll ever make.

"God please protect me from this evil man holding me captive. Send someone to find me and take me home. Amen." She prayed desperately.

Heavy footsteps alerted her to his return. Elysa had been scared on occasion, but her captor sent sharp tingles of terror through her. This wasn't the man she'd agreed to work for. It was a mystery to her who he actually was even though he introduced himself as Marty Granger.

The key turned in the lock and she stifled a scream when he entered the room. If she had ever experienced evil, it was nothing compared to this man. God help her.

***

Shadow Strong Eagle frowned when the call to Elysa went to voicemail, once again stating her voicemail box was full. Two weeks have passed and no word from her. Frank, her brother and Shadow's boss, shared his concern that something happened to her.

"Still no word from her?" Star, his sister, asked sitting next to him at the kitchen table.

"No, I'm going to Frank's. Maybe he has heard from her, if not I'll start searching for her." He said standing to leave.

"Be careful my brother." Star walked him to the door and kissed his cheek before he left.

It warmed his heart that his sister loved him, but he still felt uncomfortable letting her kiss his cheek. In their community on the reservation, only a husband and his wife shared that kind of affection.

He parked next to Frank's truck and hurried to the front door.

Frank answered after he knocked. "Hey, what are you up to?"

"I want to know if you've heard from Elysa?" He asked hopefully.

"No, and I'm worried. I can't leave Ginger to take care of all our little ones." Frank replied clearly upset.

"Let me and Hawk look for her. You and I both know something is wrong." He insisted.

"Okay, but are you sure you want Hawk to go with you?" Frank asked concerned.

"Yes, he's as good as I am at tracking and has a few skillsets I don't have. Don't worry. It's time for him to let his anger go. We'll work it out." He explained hoping Hawk would hear him out.

"Alright. Go to the office and see Abe. I'll have Hawk meet you there." Frank pulled his cell phone out.

Shadow left with a growing sense of unease. Elysa had run into a situation none of them knew about. The thought of something happening to her made him ill, and it only made him that much more determined to find her hopefully alive and well.

Chapter One

Elysa set the two suitcases and her carryon in the hospital room out of the way before turning to hug her big brother.

"How is she?" Elysa asked peeking over his shoulder.

"She had a rough time, and so did the babies, but they're recuperating nicely, as the Doc put it." Frank hugged her tightly. "How was your flight? Did you take a cab? I could've picked you up."

"Long, and you needed to be here for your family. It wasn't a big deal. How are you?" She carefully observed him.

"I'll be fine now that their conditions are improving." He replied as sadness crept into his eyes.

"What aren't you telling me?" She asked, raising an eyebrow.

"They had to give her a hysterectomy. She can't have any more babies." His eyes moistened.

"I'm sorry but look at what God has given you. She gave you two strapping baby boys. I'll bet they'll be able to work circles around you when they grow up." She teased.

"Do you wanna go down to see them while Ginger is asleep?" He asked, feeling the need to get out of the room.

"Of course! I can't wait to hold my nephews." She said, following him into the hallway.

"Sis, why is your hair pink?" He couldn't help but ask.

"Dion, my latest roommate dared me to, so I did." She shrugged.

"Only my little sister would be crazy enough to walk around with pink hair." He laughed.

"I'm glad you are entertained by my choice of hair color." She smiled as he picked up the phone to access the NICU area.

After scrubbing their hands and arms up to the elbows, Frank led Elysa to the boy's room in the NICU. The nurse had just finished bathing and feeding them as they walked into the room.

"How are you this morning Mr. Goines?" The nurse looked past him to the woman sporting neon pink hair.

"Great, this is my sister, Elysa. I'll add her name to the list of visitors allowed to be here." Frank introduced them.

"The doctor is making his rounds so I'm sure he'll be in shortly to speak to you." The nurse, Kelly, said. "Enjoy your visit."

Elysa watched her leave as Frank looked at his boys' charts.

"Well big brother, are they well enough to go to the regular nursery?" She asked touching the smaller baby's fuzzy head.

"From what the charts say, it's a good possibility." He replied as the doctor knocked on the door.

"Hello, Doc Reynolds." Frank greeted him. "This is my sister Elysa."

"Nice to make your acquaintance." He shook her hand with an interested smile.

"How are they?" Frank interrupted, agitated by the attention he paid his sister.

"I'm moving them to the regular nursery this afternoon when they have free beds for them." He replied tearing his eyes from the beautiful woman with pink hair. "All their tests have come back normal, so I don't see any reason to keep them here any longer. Their weight is just over the line we want them to be."

"That's great." Frank sighed in relief.

"I'll check on them later after they move them. Tell your wife they are healthy happy babies." He said turning to leave.

Elysa took the little boy Frank held out to her and cuddled him close. "This is Willie."

"After Will Wolf?" She looked up in surprise and giggled. "That's tempting fate big brother."

"Nah." He picked up the other twin with joy radiating from his rugged face. "This is Frankie Jr."

They cuddled the little ones for almost an hour before going back to Ginger's room.

***

Shadow stealthily moved toward the two men locked in battle. Frank had sent him to work this case, but he didn't say the two men would hook it up in the middle of the front yard.

What was the guy doing here anyhow? Why hadn't he gone to work as usual? He hired us to get pictures of the unfaithful wife with her boyfriend, so why was he home?

Moving forward, he pounced on them before they knew what happened. Shadow subdued the stronger one, then ducked as the weak one took a swing at him. When he tried the second time, Shadow put him down and cuffed him.

The minute he turned around to check on the wife, he looked into the barrel of a thirty-eight revolver. His quick reflexes allowed him to disarm the wife before she could shoot him. Whether he wanted to or not he had to cuff her as well.

The police cars screeched to a halt and the officers rushed him.

"Whoa! I'm with the security company that man hired." Shadow held his hands up leaving the gun in the waistband of his pants.

The officer grabbed the gun and cuffed him, then escorted him and the boyfriend into one patrol car and the wife and his client in the other.

After they interviewed the neighbors, the officer's drove them to the station.

Three long hours later, the lead officer released him after Frank vouched for him.

"We're sorry for the inconvenience, but we couldn't let you remain free until we had the complete story." He explained.

"No worries, I'm just glad it all worked out." Shadow shrugged.

"We're filing assault and battery charges against the men and the woman with assault with a deadly weapon." He told him.

"Good, I need to get back home, so if there's nothing else…" Shadow looked for the man's approval.

"Nope you're free to go. Thanks for providing the information you found for us. It'll go a long way when the judge charges them." He replied.

"No problem. If you need anything later, call me." Shadow handed him the business card for CFS (Charlie Foxtrot Security Inc.).

Shadow left Casper behind as he drove home. Frank told him Elysa had arrived when he'd called him earlier. He decided to stop at the hospital to check on Ginger and see if Elysa needed a ride to Frank's house.

Chapter Two

Elysa sat on the bench in Ginger's room cuddling little Frankie while Ginger fed Willie with a radiant smile on her face. Still sadness lurked in her eyes. She couldn't fathom a doctor telling her she couldn't have any more babies. That kind of news would cut deep into a person's soul.

Frank had gone downstairs to get them each a drink and snacks. Elysa knew he needed to get out of the room for a few minutes. When the door opened, he stepped inside with Shadow following close behind.

"Hey Shadow." She greeted him as her heart did a happy dance in her chest.

"Hau." He greeted her in the Lakota way.

"He's heading to the house, you wanna ride with him to get some rest> I know you're probably tired having to catch a plane out here so quickly." Frank asked observing her reaction to the Lakota man.

"I would thank you. I'll come back in the morning so you can go home and get some rest since the boys are out of the NICU." She passed Willie off to his daddy.

"I'm glad you're here to help." Ginger said while burping Frankie.

"I wouldn't pass on seeing my new family members." She assured her.

Shadow grabbed her luggage and followed her out of the room. When they reached his truck, she hopped inside while he stowed her luggage in the back.

When he buckled in, he started the engine, and they were on their way to Wolf Creek.

"Are you hungry?" He asked before they left Sheridan behind.

"Not really, I'm more tired than anything else." She replied.

"I'll bet. You had little warning that Frank and Ginger needed you here." He commented.

"I planned to be here before her last few weeks of pregnancy, but the little guys were anxious to greet the world." She said with a smile.

"They certainly surprised everyone." He replied.

Silence filled the cab again as she forced her eyes to remain open. In the end, she leaned against the door and fell asleep.

Shadow knew the minute she fell asleep when her breathing evened into a steady rhythm. A smile graced his face when a soft snore slipped from her lips. When he glanced over at her, he wished he could tangle his fingers in her long pink hair.

He almost laughed when he beheld her in Ginger's room. If he had, he most certainly would have suffered the consequences of his action.

The rest of the trip, he contemplated when to ask her for a date. First Frank had to approve, or he would walk away. For some reason that thought made his heart ache.

***

A light flickered in the dark apartment. The occupant opened the refrigerator and grabbed a beer before closing it. One long drink from the bottle eased the pain in his head.

"Let me see the pictures you have." A raspy voice insisted.

"Gimme a minute." Came the response as an envelope of pictures landed on the table.

The thud of the beer bottle hitting the trashcan broke the silent room. "Are you through? I want to see the pictures."

"Alright already!" The man grumbled.

A big beefy hand picked up the envelope and pulled out a big stack of photos.

11

Pictures of Frank Goines, his wife and sister fell onto the table as the man looked at each one. The bundle also contained pictures of Will Wolf and his entire family, the sheriff, and other townsfolk in conversation with Will and Frank.

"You sure the sister will show up when we call her?" the gruff voice asked doubtfully.

"I already talked to her. She's excited to begin her new job." The other quiet voice chuckled.

The sound of tape ripping from the dispenser sounded as the gruff man taped the pictures on the huge board on one wall of the room. Every picture involved the Wolf Creek families.

They wouldn't know what hit them after they executed the plan they'd put together. The entire thing depended on getting Elysa under their control.

"I can't wait to see the shock on their faces when they discover we're the one's targeting them." The gruff man laughed.

"As long as we don't hurt the innocent ones. Will and Frank are the only ones I want to suffer." The quiet man insisted.

"Yeah, yeah. I hear you. You take all the fun out of everything." The gruff voice grumbled.

The quiet man fell silent hiding his worry. He knew there would come a time soon when his brother would take over. At that point there would be no stopping him once he tasted the thrill of bloodshed and havoc his brother would unleash upon his enemies.

Tired from his long journey, the quiet man laid down and closed his eyes unaware his brother had plans that didn't include him during the night.

***

Shadow parked his truck in the driveway next to Hawk's truck. The two men had bar duty tonight and it was nearly time to close.

12

Shutting the engine down, he turned toward Elysa. Rather than disturb her sleep, he went to open the front door then returned to carry her upstairs to her room.

Gently placing her in the middle of the bed, he removed her shoes then covered her with a big fluffy throw blanket. He reached out to gently pull her hair away from her face before leaving to retrieve her luggage.

He sat at the table in the kitchen with a glass of water thinking of the lovely young woman upstairs. Would Frank allow him to date her? That he wouldn't know until he asked. Soon, he decided, when everything settled back to normal. Although, he knew nothing was ever normal around Ginger.

A smile graced his rugged face when he remembered their first meeting. He thought Larry would die laughing when he called her Shappa, (red thunder). Steam rolled out of Ginger's ears as she stormed into the kitchen of the bar.

The door opened as Hawk and Justice came in from work.

"Hey y'all. Heads up, Elysa is in the guestroom asleep." He informed them.

"Thanks for the warning. See y'all in the morning." Justice stepped on the stairs.

Hawk made a huge sandwich and poured himself a large glass of milk. He sat down across from Shadow refraining from talking to him.

"How was work." Shadow asked, not expecting an answer from him.

"Same ol,' same ol'." How's Ginger?" He asked.

"They're okay. The twins are out of the NICU." Shadow answered standing on his feet. "I'm going to lock up."

"I'll do it when I'm done." He insisted before taking a large bite out of the sandwich.

"In that case, I'll see you in the morning." Shadow moved toward the staircase as Hawk downed half the glass of milk in one swallow.

Shadow slipped between the sheets of his bed with sadness wrapping around his heart. He missed his blood brother. Even though he made the right decision, Hawk's love for his sister put a wedge in their friendship.

It didn't matter that Shadow's intentions to save him from heartbreak when he gave Trace permission to date Star.

Hawk hadn't said more than a dozen words to him other than when they had to work together, then it was business.

Shadow rolled to his side willing his body to relax and tried to clear his mind. Tomorrow he would try again to ease his blood brother's hurt.

Chapter Three

Tiny shafts of sunlight slowly crept across the room chasing the shadow of night away. Tiny dust particles seemingly danced in the spotlight as the beams climbed the bedside reaching past the obstacle hampering its journey.

Elysa squinted her closed eyes when the bright light bathed her face in its warmth. Her automatic response to stretch seized her body, although her slumbering muscles resisted it felt too good to stop.

Her mouth opened to one last deep yawn as she pushed the covers off and hurried into the bathroom to get ready for the day. Frank needed a break no matter how much he protested.

She smiled at the memory of his face when she informed him, he wasn't in the Military any longer. Whether he wanted to admit it or not, his attitude mirrored their father's. He often forgot his children weren't soldiers.

Rushing through her shower and dressing, she hurried downstairs where she knew Shadow was waiting for her. With a quick look at the clock, she knew it was later than she'd originally planned.

"Hey! Sorry I overslept." She greeted Shadow as he moved toward her from the den.

"No worries, are you ready?" He asked with admiration in his eyes.

"Yes." She nodded as he put his hand on her back to lead her from the house.

After driving down the block to the diner, Shadow helped her from the truck. He guided her to the table furthest from the door.

"Good morning, what can I get y'all to drink?" Sandra asked.

"I'll have a coffee, two eggs over medium, a short stack, three slices of bacon and a bowl of fruit." Elysa held back a chuckle watching amazement flash through his eyes.

"How about you, Shadow?" She asked with a smile.

"Coffee, western omelet, with biscuits and gravy." He ordered with a slight flush coloring his high cheekbones.

The woman left after pouring their coffee assuring them their food would arrive shortly.

They settled into a light conversation avoiding any sad situations or personal subjects. Elysa found her companion to be funny and a man of strong belief's.

The server appeared laden with plates of food. After putting it on the table she asked if we needed anything else before leaving them to dig in.

Their conversation became stilted as they ate until the bell over the door drew their attention. Josh stepped inside to order his lunch early because of his workload.

When his eyes landed on Elysa a smile broke out over his handsome face. He moved toward them when Elysa jumped from her seat and threw herself into his arms.

"When did you get back?" He asked in surprise.

"Yesterday. I stayed with Frank and Ginger until last night. Shadow brought me home." She said, leading him back to the table.

"Hello Shadow. How are you?" He asked, noting his furrowed brow.

"I am well." Shadow replied.

"Sit down and have breakfast with us." She insisted.

"Nah, I've got a desk full of paperwork waiting for me. Y'all have a good day." He refused politely.

Shadow watched him leave before his eyes fell on Elysa's sad face.

"So, you and Josh?" He asked, wondering what went on between them.

"Josh and I dated a few months but realized early in the relationship we weren't meant to be together. We make better friends than lovers. He has different goals in life than I do." She explained.

"Okay. Are you ready to go?" He stood to help her from the chair.

"I need the ladies' room first." She allowed him to help her.

While she was in the restroom, he paid the bill and waited by the door for her. When she arrived, he opened the door and escorted her to his truck.

Minutes later, they were on their way to Sheridan. Elysa peppered him with questions about the reservation and his home there. Surprised by his status in the village he lived in, she had more questions.

"Why did you leave that position?" She couldn't believe he turned down being the chief.

After a moment of indecision, he felt if he wanted more with the lovely woman by his side, he would have to share everything with her.

"I couldn't bear to stay there any longer. I was married, but another man murdered her and my unborn child." He explained taking a much-needed breath. "Six months later, my mother passed away too. Everywhere I went, their memory haunted me. I finally left it all behind and wound up in Wolf Creek."

"I'm so sorry for your loss. Did they catch the man responsible?" She asked.

"No one knows yet, Star recently told me she witnessed what he did to my wife. I haven't decided what I'm going to do about it yet. He may solve the problem before I do since he's searching for Star." His knuckles turned white as he gripped the steering wheel.

Silence filled the cab when he turned into a hospital parking area slot and cut the engine.

He hurried around the truck to help her out then they strolled into the hospital.

They disappeared into the building unaware of diabolical eyes following their every move. Soon they would find out just how cruel he could be.

They didn't heed the warning that day and he paid the price for it. Retribution would be swift and excruciating, the fact that he would enjoy every moment of their torture was beside the point.

He turned the engine to his beat-up old van and drove toward Wolf Creek. Time to stake out Frank's home and plan the plethora of surprises leading up to the ultimate ending.

Chapter Four

Frank looked up when Elysa came in with Shadow following close behind. "Hey Ladybug."

"How are y'all this morning?" She asked as her gaze fell on the twins sleeping in their little beds.

"Ready for a shower and some sleep." Frank yawned.

"I'll give you a ride back since you're too tired to drive." Shadow offered.

"Thanks. I'll need to go to the ranch to see how far along the builders are with the house. Hopefully, they'll have it ready by the time Doc releases them." Frank accepted.

"Cowboy, you need to get your rest first." Ginger's eyes narrowed at him.

"I'm not working. I'll just see their progress so I can figure out if we can move in or cram all of us in our little bedroom." He explained. "I promise Red."

"Shadow, you heard him. Don't let him do anything after he looks at the house." Ginger insisted.

"Okay Shappa." He grinned as Frank chuckled.

"That ain't funny!" She hissed. "Go away!"

Frank kissed her red cheek and left the women alone to talk.

"So, what's with you and Shadow?" Ginger couldn't contain her curiosity.

"What do you mean? He just offered to drive me home and back here this morning. Why?" Elysa didn't understand.

"All right. If you don't want to tell me that's fine." Ginger huffed crossing her arms.

"There is nothing going on Ginger. He's just being nice." She insisted.

"If you say so." Ginger said as Willie let her know he was hungry.

Elysa handed the little guy to his mother as Frankie stirred.

"I swear all these two do is eat." Ginger grumbled.

"That's natural. They're growing boys." Elysa said picking Frankie up to cuddle him until it was his turn to eat.

"Truthfully, I hope the house is finished so we can move in the day I'm outta here." Ginger sighed.

"It'll all work out Ginger. When they're finished, I'll round the ladies up and we'll get you all moved in." She promised.

***

Shadow parked in front of Frank's new log house. The enormous structure revealed his boss's desire for children. If he read Ginger right, she agreed with him.

Frank hopped from Shadow's truck as the contractor stepped out onto the wrap around porch. Shadow followed behind, remaining silent while he familiarized himself with his surroundings. In his observation he could defend the house if needed.

His attention turned to Frank and his contractor, Danny, discussing the completion date.

"All we have to do is hang the light fixtures and paint the downstairs. When we're finished, the floor crew will be in to lay the carpets, tile, and wood floors. I'd say it'll be ready to move in by then." Danny explained.

"Great! I'll leave you to go back to work." Frank sent him a pleased smile.

"Are you ready?" Shadow asked.

"Yes, I need some sleep." Frank said, getting into Shadow's truck. "Ginger will be happy when I tell her the news."

What are you going to do with all those bedrooms upstairs?" He asked curiously.

Shadow caught the fleeting sadness in Frank's eyes as he answered. "I hope to fill it with more children, but right now I don't know."

"Why not?" Shadow asked even more curious.

"It's nothing I can't deal with. Thanks for being our chauffeur the last few days." Frank changed the subject.

"It's no problem. I needed something to do anyhow, since I've been taking turns watching over Star." He shrugged.

"Still no word on him?" Frank asked.

"No. Kevin is keeping in contact with several people, but no one has seen him or his friends." Shadow shook his head as he parked in the driveway.

"I'm sure they'll give up looking." Frank said.

"No, they won't. I know the man and he doesn't give up easily." Shadow disagreed."

"Well, just watch your sixes." Frank yawned as they walked into the house.

Kevin Bright Sky looked up when they entered the house. "Hau."

"Hau. What are you up to?" Shadow asked.

"Waiting for the phone to ring." He sighed.

"You always hated waiting around for your cases to work out." Shadow grinned.

"I'm not the only one who's like that. Hawk is worse than I am." He defended himself as his stomach growled loudly.

"Let's get lunch. I'm buying." Shadow suggested.

"In that case let's go." He grinned when he heard Frank mumbling about using English around him.

The two men snickered as they left. Instead of driving, they chose to enjoy the cool day and walk to the bar. They discussed alternatives to Star's safety.

After they gave Larry their order, they sat down with the soda they preferred to liquor. Neither of them chose to ignore the laws of their ancestors. Anyone nearby could hear their conversation if they wanted to listen, but they wouldn't understand the Lakota language.

"I'll be glad when we can get Falcon and his friends in custody." Shadow sighed.

"We will. I've sent fliers out to every law enforcement office in the surrounding area. Someone will report them." Kevin assured him.

They enjoyed their lunch then went back to Frank's house. Kevin sat at the table learning how to use email. Shadow chuckled when Kevin threw his hands in the air and grabbed the newspaper sitting next to it.

"Giving up so soon?" Shadow asked grinning.

"I'd rather read a newspaper. I never did understand the need for all that electronic stuff." He said flipping the paper open.

Shadow looked up as Frank entered the room. "Hey, you didn't sleep very long."

"I'll be okay. Would you drive me to the hospital and bring Elysa home?" Frank asked.

"Absolutely." Shadow stood and moved toward the door.

They discussed several cases Frank's men were working on during the drive to Sheridan.

Chapter Five

Marty jumped when a car backfired in the parking lot of the motel where he stayed. He calmed down when the car backfired again, and he knew it wasn't gunfire.

With a clear head, he hoped that maybe his brother would keep quiet today. But eventually he would begin badgering him and his headache would return.

After a shower and a shave, he packed everything up and stowed it in the trunk of the SUV he drove. He dropped the key to the room off at the front desk, then drove to the nearest diner.

The sweet smell of pastries mixed with coffee and bacon made his mouth water. The server led him to a corner booth in the back and took his order.

"About time you got up to feed us." Paul, his brother, grabbed his cup of coffee.

"I hoped you would leave me alone today." Marty's shoulders sagged.

"There is too much planning to do. You need to call Elysa and tell her when we'll need her to start working for us." Paul told him.

The server brought his order and refilled his coffee before asking if he needed anything else.

Marty told her no and dug into the large plate of food in front of him.

Paul fell silent as they ate carefully going over the plan he had. Marty was too weak to execute the plan alone. Not to mention the fact that he didn't like to torture people.

His little stint in the military taught him nothing about the life he had to lead now. The life Wolf and Bear had forced on him darkened his soul beyond the darkness that already resided there. Retribution for their interference lay on the horizon and it would be swift and painful for both of them.

***

Elysa set breakfast on the table for Shadow and his friend Kevin. The man was gorgeous, but she was head over heels in love with Shadow. If her brother knew, he'd blow a gasket, so she kept it to herself. However, there was no reason she couldn't admire him from afar. Besides, what her brother didn't know wouldn't hurt him.

Since she'd left for New York to work for that fashion magazine, she found it wasn't as exciting as she thought it would be. A good friend introduced her to an acquaintance at her annual Halloween party. His name was Martin Granger, the famous reporter who had secretly photographed the worst terror cells in the Middle East. When someone blew their cover, it led to their capture, torture, and the death of his photographer.

The government sent in one of its most elite SEAL teams to bring him home. The information Marty possessed helped them take down one of the most ruthless leaders in the area.

After that ordeal was over, he decided he would turn his focus toward home. During his conversations with Elysa, he convinced her to become his photojournalist on his latest project. The untold stories of the homeless around the USA.

"Where'd you go Elysa?" Shadow asked, drawing her out of her thoughts.

"Just thinking about my next project," She said excitedly.

"Tell me about it." He asked.

"Promise you won't say anything to Frank. I need to tell him myself." She insisted.

"My lips are sealed." He replied with a grin.

"I quit the fashion magazine before I left New York." She began. "I've accepted a job with a journalist telling the stories of the homeless all over the U.S."

"That sounds dangerous." He commented surprised she would accept that kind of job. "Homeless people sometimes are suffering from schizophrenia or other diseases."

"I'll be fine. Marty will protect me." She responded. "He's finishing his last assignment in the Middle East, then wants to stay in the U.S. and work."

Shadow suspected there was a reason the man suddenly decided not to travel out of the country anymore. "Why did he change?"

"He was captured and tortured until one of the SEAL teams rescued him." She explained. "Marty doesn't want to wind up in that situation again."

"You should tell Frank," He said.

"Not yet, and you and Kevin better not say a word." She warned them. "I mean it, this is my life and I'll live it the way I see fit."

"But..." He opened his mouth and closed it when her eyes went cold, dark, and deadly.

"Don't say another word!" She insisted. "Another thing, if you'd leave Star alone, she'd be happier. You gotta let her live her life the way she wants."

"Now you're getting into my business." He growled. "She is my sister."

"She's also an adult." Elysa countered. "I don't know what it is with brothers. They always butt into where they don't belong."

"Everybody take a breath." Kevin interrupted.

"See! Even Kevin is interfering!" She huffed. "What is it, in your genes or something?"

"Hey, I'm only trying to keep the peace. There's no call for either of you to get angry." Kevin spoke, raising his hands in surrender.

"Don't worry, I'm leaving before I get any angrier."
She turned to go.

"Where are you going?" Shadow couldn't help but
ask.

"Not that it's any of your business, but I'm meeting
Star and Samantha at Frank and Ginger's new house."
She hissed.

"We should go too, just in case they need more
help." Shadow insisted as he stood to follow her.

"It's a free country, do whatever you want." Elysa
picked up her dish and put it in the dishwasher.

Minutes later she left driving Frank's truck since the
SUV he bought for Ginger was at the hospital waiting
to take the little family home.

When she parked next to Samantha's SUV, she took
a deep cleansing breath and let the argument with
Shadow go. If she held onto it, the ladies would insist
she tell them what was wrong. That subject would
remain her secret until she revealed it on her own terms.

The day seemed to fly by even though Samantha
went into labor and Will rushed her to Doc's in town.
Star questioned her about the tension between Shadow
and her.

Unbeknownst to Elysa, Frank stepped into the house
and heard her explaining her new job to Star. When he
bellowed, she wasn't taking the job, Star made a hasty
exit to help Ginger with the babies.

Frank followed Elysa through to the front door
arguing with her until she turned to him and told him to
leave her alone.

"I'm a big girl Frankie! I can take care of myself!
You don't get to run my life for me. If I want to accept
a job, no matter what it is, I'll take it." She insisted
angrily.

Ginger watched them as they approached the SUV and knew by the look on their faces the siblings were having a difference of opinion.

Elysa picked little Willie up and carried him inside feeling instant calm holding the little guy.

With all the help from friends, neighbors and employees of Charlie Foxtrot Security, Inc. The house was completely set up for them by sundown. Elysa took the room furthest away from the stairs. Ginger insisted they put the babies in the new bassinets next to her bed so she could be up with them in the middle of the night.

Elysa slipped between the sheets completely spent. Arguing with her brother just added to her weariness. He would never understand she had the right to do as she pleased now.

Chapter Six

Marty drove toward Denver after arranging to meet Elysa at the airport in Houston. At least that was the plan until Paul changed everything.

"We're going to meet her in Denver before she gets on the connecting flight to Houston." Paul said. "We need to find a place between Wolf Creek and Casper."

"Why the change in the plans?" Marty asked as the knot in his stomach grew painful.

"The element of surprise. We'll snatch her when she changes planes. With so many people in the terminal, no one will pay attention. Don't worry, I've got this." Paul insisted.

"I worry you're going to hurt her." Marty said anxiously.

"Elysa is the bait, Marty. We'll use her to get Bear." Paul reminded him. "You need to get with the program. Stop feeling sorry for her, she's just a means to an end."

"She never did anything to us! It ain't right to use her like this. Bear and Wolf are the ones who had me thrown into the brig!" Marty slammed his hand against the steering wheel.

"Maybe you should be the one to keep quiet. I'm tired of arguing with you over this!" Paul sighed angrily.

"You wouldn't even be here if it weren't for me." Marty growled.

"Are you sure? Seems to me I've had your back since the day our father killed mother." Paul asked.

"Please don't bring all that up." Marty's throat constricted.

He loved his mother and missed her terribly. That was also the day Marty committed his first murder. The attorney helped him obtain a self-defense verdict after producing evidence of severe abuse to them and their mother. Somehow, he'd managed to keep Paul quiet during the trial, but afterward he became almost uncontrollable.

Out of desperation, he joined the military and wound up in boot camp with Will Wolf and Frank Goines. Now he would hunt them down and get his revenge.

"Snap out of it! We're at the half-way mark. Let's start looking for abandoned rural homes." Paul shouted.

"Okay." Marty said quietly. Deep down he knew this was the end game for them. How to stop it? He had no idea anymore.

***

Elysa grabbed her purse and camera equipment as Frank took her luggage out of the trunk. With each step into the terminal at the Sheridan Airport, that deep gut feeling intensified. With a heavy sigh, he had to try one more time to get his sister to see reason. "Sis, I love you, but I have a bad feeling about this."

"Frankie, you've always got a bad feeling about anything I want to do. I know you love me and that you promised Daddy to watch over me, but you gotta understand, I'm almost twenty-six and it's my decision to make if I want to or not. Now let's not argue anymore. I don't want to leave angry." She turned her big blue eyes on him.

"Well, I guess I should be grateful you did away with the pink hair. You look more like my little sister now. Forgive me for being overprotective. I just worry." He relented.

"I know Frankie. Marty will watch over me." She swallowed the lump in her throat.

"Give me his number just in case." Frank asked again.

"No. You'll just call him and stir up a hornet's nest. I don't need you threatening him. I'm not marrying the man. I'm only taking pictures of his subjects." She shook her head as the attendant announced the plane was boarding.

"I love you Ladybug." Frank hugged her.

"I love you too Frankie. Take care of my nephews." She said as she turned to leave.

Frank watched her leave worried about what might happen to her. He left the airport after her plane took off and went to his office. Abe could find out about Marty Granger.

Anger washed over him that he hadn't already run a background check on the man. Even though he was busy with the twins and Ginger, it was no excuse for not checking into his past. If he had more concerns, he would find her and bring her home.

He pulled into the parking garage next to his office and went inside. It was time to get to work.

***

Elysa settled back into her seat thinking about her brother and Shadow's warnings. Didn't they understand she could take care of herself. It escaped their notice she did fine while living in New York City.

She closed her eyes to ease the ache in her head. Arguing with her brother always brough a headache on. Mostly because she couldn't think faster than he could. That's what made him so successful in everything he did. She was proud of him, but just once she wished he would be proud of her choices rather than try to control her.

Shadow's handsome face appeared in her thoughts. Someday she hoped he would see her for more than his boss's sister. A smile graced her face when she realized how similar he was to Frank. What were the odds she'd find someone as stubborn as her brother?

The seat belt sign came on as the pilot announced their descent to the airport in Denver. Snapping her belt securely around her, the excited feeling returned and so did the niggling warning in the back of her mind she chose to ignore.

Soon they disembarked from the plane, and she hurried to catch the connecting flight to Houston. As she approached the gate the attendant made the announcement that due to a storm threatening Houston, they cancelled the flight.

Disappointment washed over her as she made her way toward the help desk to get accommodation for the night. She joined the lengthy line of angry passengers waiting for the same vouchers.

When the line moved down to her, she managed to secure a room at a rundown motel near the airport. All the others were filled to capacity.

She stepped out of the terminal to rain and high winds. The air was cold suggesting the rain might turn to snow. Looking toward the lanes where cabs waited for passengers to hail them.

Lifting her hand, she clutched her luggage hoping to catch one. When the cab stopped in front of her, she hopped in while he put her luggage in the trunk. After giving him the name of the motel, she sat back to enjoy the short ride. Her stomach protested being empty as they passed a small diner and he pulled into the motel lot.

The place looked like it should have been condemned a long time ago. However, it was the only room left near the airport.

The driver unloaded her rolling suitcase and accepted her payment before leaving. Elysa placed the voucher on the desk and received a room key from the manager.

"I'm sorry the only room we have left is on the back side of the motel." He informed her.

"I guess it will have to do. I don't know when they'll have another flight to Houston." She sighed, accepting her situation.

After signing the paperwork, she hurried to drop her luggage off at the room, then ran across the street to the diner in the chilly rain.

In no hurry, she enjoyed the hot chocolate and chili that heated her chilled insides. After paying the bill, she ran across the road to the motel and into her room. She locked the door behind her and took a long hot shower.

She slipped between the sheets after checking for critters and cleanliness then turned the lights off for a good night's sleep.

Chapter Seven

Shadow had just returned from a long assignment for Frank. During the few days he was gone, he tried to phone Elysa, but her phone went to voicemail again, informing him the voicemail box was full. He decided to visit his sister in the morning then if Elysa didn't answer, he would talk to Frank.

Shadow tossed and turned in his bed trying to wake himself from the nightmare holding him captive.

In the dream he called Elysa worried something was wrong with her.

Just before it went to voicemail, he heard her sleepy voice. "Hello?"

"Elysa, are you okay?" He asked relieved to hear her voice.

"Yes. Why are you calling so late?" She sounded annoyed.

"I had a bad feeling." He said with his voice laced with concern.

"I'm okay. Now you should rest, you silly man." She told him.

Shadow sat up sweating profusely when he heard a crash. The terrified scream from Elysa chilled him to the bone.

He grabbed his cell and swore when he realized he forgot to charge it. Grumbling, he plugged it in and went downstairs to get a drink of water.

Hawk sat at the table with Kevin discussing the situation Star found herself in and how to find Falcon and his friends.

"Man, you look like someone beat you with an ugly stick." Hawk snorted.

"Can it." Shadow said crossing to the refrigerator and grabbing a bottle of water.

"What's wrong Shadow?" Kevin asked.

"I have a bad feeling something is wrong with Elysa. I forgot to charge my phone so I can't call her." He explained.

"Elysa's a big girl. She can take care of herself." Hawk said.

"I know, but it doesn't stop me from worrying about her." Shadow said going back upstairs hoping it had enough of a charge to restart it.

***

Marty waited an hour after Elysa's light in her room went out. The girl had no idea he'd followed her from the airport. He felt fortunate they cancelled the flight to Houston. Now he had a little more time to cover his tracks after he grabbed her.

Carefully picking the lock on the door, he quickly slipped inside without a sound. An evil smile graced his face when he heard her soft snore. Elated that she had no idea he had entered the room, he quickly crossed to her bedside ready with the cloth laced with chloroform.

A faint sound reached Elysa's ears as she opened her eyes. The shadow standing over her moved quickly covering her mouth with a cloth. The sweet odor of the chloroform ended her struggle almost as soon as it began.

***

Shadow met with Hawk in Abe's office. There were monitors everywhere. He and the two techs Frank hired to help him were busily typing on their keyboards as data filled the screens.

"Come on in fellas." Abe said looking up from the screen on his desk.

"Do you have any information for us before we head out?" Shadow asked while Hawk stood stiffly behind him with his arms crossed.

The man was clearly unhappy to be working with Shadow again. Everyone knew Hawk was in love with Star, Shadow's sister. The fact that she and Trace were now married didn't help the situation any.

Jealousy slowly ate away at the friendship born on the reservation where they grew up together. Friendships like that were rare and when something happens to put a wedge in it, nothing is ever the same.

Abe gave them what little he had, which wasn't much, and told them they were still searching for her.

They left for the airport with a heaviness between them. Once on board, the plane taxied down the runway and left Sheridan behind.

Shadow looked at his blood brother and said, "Don't you think it's about time you forgave me for letting Star marry Trace?"

"Why should I? You knew how I felt and ignored my requests." Hawk frowned.

"Star fell in love with Trace almost from the minute they met. I could see the connection between them even before they knew it themselves." Shadow explained again.

"You didn't even give me a chance." Hawk growled.

"Clearly trying to save you from heartbreak didn't work. Star has only ever loved you as a brother." Shadow sighed.

"That's why you wouldn't let me date her?" Hawk asked.

"Yes. If we're going to work together, to find Elysa, you need to get over yourself. Star is a happily married mother now; you have to let it go. We've been blood brothers since we were old enough to understand what that means. I for one don't want to throw that away." Shadow said.

"You're right. I shouldn't let our friendship go. Star's happy and that's all I should be concerned about." Hawk relented.

"We need to figure out how we'll proceed after we land." Shadow changed the subject.

"Abe said she never boarded her flight to Houston. We should start with the security tapes at the airport." Hawk suggested.

"What if they don't allow us to see them." Shadow's brows furrowed.

"I'll call Gator. He'll get permission from his contacts at the FBI to get us in the door." Hawk assured him.

The pilot announced their approach to the airport in Denver.

Chapter Eight

After the plane landed, they found the security department and began watching the tapes without any hassle.

While reviewing the video, Hawk said. "Stop. Go back slowly."

The technician did as instructed.

"There. That guy is following her. He obviously knows where the cameras are. See how he keeps his head down and the hat over his eyes." Hawk said.

"Do you have another angle we can look at?" Shadow asked.

"Surely." The technician typed information into his computer.

"Please email this to this address. Our technician can enhance it for us." Hawk handed him his business card.

Thirty minutes later, Shadow had the directions to the motel the airline sent her to. After picking up the SUV Abe arranged for them, he parked in the motel parking lot.

An older man looked up when they walked inside. "Can I help you fellas?"

"We're looking for this woman. Have you seen her?" Hawk showed him the picture Abe placed in her file.

"Sure did. Something happened to her, and I called the police when I discovered her belongings still in the room. I have all her things stored in my office. I was beginning to think no one would come and ask for them. There's some mighty high-priced camera equipment in there." The man explained.

"May we see the room?" Shadow asked as his worry intensified.

"I don't see a problem. The police released the room a day later and we've cleaned it since then. I don't know if it will help you any." The man replied grabbing the key.

Hawk accepted the key and walked away leaving Shadow to follow him. When they reached the room Shadow said. "This is the worst place to put a single woman. There's no clear line of sight from the office, and it's the room closest to the alley."

"Let's assume the motel had no more vacancies. And if this man followed her, he had a perfect set up to kidnap her." Hawk suggested.

As the manager said, there wasn't anything in the room for them to find, so they returned the key and gathered Elysa's luggage. They put her things in the back of the SUV.

"She left her purse and cell phone too." Shadow sighed.

"We'll find her. Don't lose hope now." Hawk insisted.

"Let's just hope Abe can get us a good picture of the man following her." Shadow said. "Let's go talk to the officers who investigated her disappearance."

Hawk agreed and drove them to the police station. They finally ushered them to an interrogation room to wait for the detectives who the chief assigned the job to them.

Detectives James Wallace and Juan Sanchez entered shortly after the two men sat down.

Detective Wallace placed a thin file on the table as he sat down.

"What do you know about Elysa Goines disappearance." Shadow asked before the man could ask the question."

"First, why are you asking?" Det. Sanchez asked suspiciously.

Hawk slid their business card toward the man and explained why they were there.

"I've heard nothing but good things about CFS." Det. Wallace read the card. "There was a short struggle judging from how we found the bed clothes on the floor. It's impossible to fingerprint the room because of the traffic in and out of there."

"So, you found no clues at all?" Shadow slumped back into the chair.

"The perpetrator picked the lock to gain entry. We can only assume whoever kidnapped Elysa drugged her. No one heard any screams of the few travelers still remaining in their rooms. There weren't any cameras outside the building and with the alley being next to the room, I'm quite sure they were in and out in under five minutes." Det. Sanchez informed them.

"May we have a copy of that report?" Hawk asked.

"I don't see why not. We have no leads so maybe you'll have better luck." Det. Wallace said, handing the file to his partner.

"So, this, Elysa is the sister to your boss?" Det. Wallace asked.

"Yes." Hawk replied.

"Since she is his sister, I'm sure he sent his best men to find her. Am I correct?" His face remained passive.

"Every employee at CFS excels in their area of expertise. That said, tracking and surveillance is our area." Shadow said as Det. Sanchez returned with the copy of their file.

"Thank you for this." Hawk accepted the file.

"All we ask is that you keep us informed. We'll manage arrests and such." Det. Wallace responded.

"We will." Shadow stood to leave.

When they got into the truck, Hawk's stomach rumbled.

"I'm hungry too." Shadow said grinning.

Chapter Nine

Elysa scratched another mark on the root cellar wall. The cold of the cold dirt floor seeped through the flimsy mattress thrown against the wall. The only light came from the cracks in the door and so did the rain.

Being underground meant the temperature inside the cellar was slightly warmer than outside. Only slightly.

She sat on the mattress with the thread bare blanket Marty covered her with after his brother Paul had punished her for complaining about the accommodations. She shivered as her mind replayed the punishment.

Paul was a ruthless beast. If he said something to her, she had better comply, or he would retaliate. After he finished, he left her crying in pain. Thank God he hadn't done the unthinkable to her. Saving herself for marriage was tough, but she wouldn't just give herself like that to any man except the man she would marry.

Marty came in shortly after Paul's punishment to clean her wounds and give her food.

"You shouldn't anger him like that." Marty shook his head as he bandaged her wounds.

"Are you twins?" She asked mentally observing that not only were they identical, but they wore the same clothes.

"You could say that." He replied as he gave her a lunchbox like you would find in a school cafeteria.

"Can't you stop him from hurting me?" She asked hopefully.

"Paul is the stronger of the two of us. I can only do so much before he gets angry at me." He explained.

"How come you didn't mention him when we talked in New York?" She asked.

"It isn't important now. Just do what he says, and you'll be okay." He turned to leave.

Elysa watched him leave the cellar and heard the padlock click. Tears gathered in her eyes as she ate the cold bologna and cheese sandwich. The bottle of water was small but quenched her thirst.

After relieving herself in the small bucket he provided her with, she laid on the mattress again, wishing the pain from his brutal attack would ease.

Soon she fell asleep hiccupping from crying so hard.

***

Marty stomped into the house so angry he could barely see straight. "Why did you hurt her so bad?"

"She needed to know we ain't putting up with any disobedience from her. Besides, you yourself have tortured people so what's the difference?"

"She didn't do anything to us! Wolf and Bear are the ones we want!" Marty yelled holding his head.

"Go lay down and take a nap." Paul insisted.

Marty fell into bed after taking a handful of pills to stop the coming migraine. Deep down he knew his brother had grown strong enough to take over. When the time came, he wondered if he would survive.

***

Frank picked up his cell phone when it rang. "Hello?"

"Hey Bear, Shadow and I are heading back. We've gone as far as we can here in Denver. Abe is gonna have to do his computer voodoo to find a trail. We have the police report and Elysa's luggage, purse, and camera equipment she left at the hotel." Hawk told him.

"When are you arriving?" Frank asked.

"We should be at the airport by two p.m." He replied.

"I'll be there to pick you up. We can talk with Abe when I bring you to the office." Frank said.

"Will do." Hawk ended the call.

"Did they find her?" Ginger's sleepy voice asked.

"No, I've gotta pick them up at two. Do you want me to ask Abigail if she will help you while I'm gone?" He asked.

"No, she went back to school today." Ginger shook her head. "Call Sandra, since she and Dillon got married, she offered to help me."

"Okay. It's funny that Heather and Sandra are so different." Frank voiced his observation.

"I'm kinda glad Heather left. Dillon is so much happier now. Before he couldn't come to visit without a huge fight. We can visit him now that she's gone." Ginger said.

"I'll make the call then I need to head out." He said kissing her.

"Be safe and don't worry too much. Elysa has a good head on her shoulders. She won't do anything to cause herself any harm." Ginger tried to ease his worry.

"Let's hope so." He said as he walked out of the room.

After kissing his large family while they slept, Frank called and arranged for Sandra to help Ginger. He hopped in his truck and left for the airport. By his calculations, he would make it just in time.

He prayed all the way to Sheridan that God would help Elysa and keep her safe. His heart was so heavy with worry he could barely think straight.

Shadow and Hawk were waiting for him when he arrived.

"Tell me everything." Frank insisted as he drove away from the terminal.

Abe looked up when Frank stepped into the door of his office with Shadow and Hawk following closely behind.

"This is the picture of the man following Elysa." Abe said, handing the photo over to Frank.

When he swore, Hawk looked over his shoulder and joined Frank in swearing.

"What's going on? Who is this man?" Shadow asked when Frank passed the photo over to him.

"The threat we've waited on all these years to make his move." Frank growled. "Abe, find him. His name is Marty Durango. He tricked Elysa by calling himself Marty Granger."

"D.J. Start looking into financials. I'll try tracking him from the airport." Abe said while his fingers flew over the keyboard in front of him.

"Let's leave them to it. I gotta warn Wolf." Frank said, leaving the room.

"Tell me about this man." Shadow insisted as he followed his boss.

"Hawk will tell you." Frank said as he closed his office door.

Shadow and Hawk went into the break room.

"I'm waiting." Shadow said.

"This whole thing started in boot camp." Hawk sighed as he told him the story. "When they sentenced him to the brig, he threatened Frank and Will. Told them he'd get even with them for testifying against him. It didn't matter that the court found him guilty."

"So, the guy is a phycho." Shadow said.

"That's one way to describe him. Sometimes we wondered about him. He seemed calm until we went into battle. That's when he became a ruthless killer. Being a glory hound, his actions that last mission before Will resigned, Durango gave our position away and we lost two good men that day. We also almost lost Will. The worst part of it, the hostage died because we couldn't get to her." Hawk explained.

"In other words, we need to find her yesterday." Shadow's jaw twitched in anger.

"You have feelings for her, don't you?" Hawk asked raising one brow.

"It's complicated." Shadow shrugged.

"Oh, come off it. You love her I can see it in your eyes." Hawk insisted.

"Yes. Okay. I admit it. Why wouldn't she listen to all of our warnings?" He asked, trying to find the answer.

"She's independent and won't listen to anyone. Like Frank." Hawk said when Abe called them back to his office.

Chapter Ten

Elysa watched as Marty threw another mattress down across from her. "Who's that for?"

"You'll see." He said before leaving again.

She drew her knees up and rested her chin on them. Not that she wanted company because that meant someone else was in her shoes.

Just when she thought she didn't have any tears left, more slipped from her puffy eyes. She'd been here for three weeks so far. What they had planned she had no idea.

She lost count of how many times she berated herself for not listening to Shadow and Frank. They warned her more than once that she was walking into a dangerous situation, but did she listen? Nope and now look at her, locked in a dirty damp root cellar with a thin mat to sleep on and a bucket for her necessities.

When would she ever learn to heed others warnings? Why did she have to be so stubborn? Being the baby of the family had made her reckless because her father or brother would always come to the rescue and save the day. This time she worried that her brother was the reason she found herself locked away where no one would find her.

"If I ever get out of this, I'll listen to my brother's advice." She muttered to herself stretching out onto the mat before sleep overtook her.

***

Will listened to Frank as his friend paced the floor of his den.

"So, you think Durango has her?" Will wanted confirmation before deciding what to do.

"So far all we know is Durango followed her out of the airport terminal. Abe has his entire department tracing every lead they find on Durango."

"Are you sure it's Marty?" Will asked.

"See for yourself." Frank pointed to the file on Will's coffee table.

"We all knew this day would come. It's time to figure out what to do." Will laid the picture back on the file.

"I don't even know if she's still alive. Until he contacts me, I have no choice but to wait for his call." Frank sat down.

"You know I have your back. Let me know what you want me to do." Will said.

"I know you do, and I appreciate it." Frank sighed.

"I'd say it's gonna be okay, but we don't know that for sure." Will said truthfully.

"I'm going home. Sandra is helping Ginger and needs to go home too." Frank stood to leave. "I'll keep you posted."

***

Shadow knocked on the door of his sister's house. While waiting, he thought back to a time before he left her alone on the reservation with their father. How could he have left her behind like that. He'd forgotten her gift of calming him down when he dove off the emotional cliff of grief.

Those were dark days at the time, and she always had the right words to say to him. Although she asked him to stay, she let him go without an argument. For that he would forever be grateful to her, yet he felt the pain of guilt for the trials she suffered in his absence.

"Han, *Ohanzee*." She greeted him in Lakota as she opened the door.

"Hau. *Winchapi*." He replied stepping into her home.

"Have you found Elysa?" She wasted no time asking.

"We know who took her, but no clue of where he's holding her." Shadow shook his head.

"Elysa is a smart and strong young woman. She'll hang in there until you can rescue her." Star showed him into the kitchen where little Allen sat in the bouncy seat on the table playing with his toes.

"From what Hawk told me the man is a total psycho." Shadow replied tickling the baby.

"I've prayed like the preacher has taught me. You will find her. Until then, God will watch over her." Star looked at him to be sure he understood.

"I hope your prayers are answered my sister." He commented.

"Will you stay for dinner?" She asked.

"Yes. Where's Trace?" He asked, looking around.

"He's out training the colt Cinnamon had last year." She told him.

"I've gotta see this." He grinned.

"Be nice, *Ohanzee*!" She swatted at him making the baby giggle.

"I'll return when Trace comes in." He left her tending to Allen.

Trace finally got the bridle on Little Bit and led him around the corral for a short time. When he spotted Shadow, he led her inside to the freshly cleaned stall.

"What's going on?" Trace asked when Shadow appeared at the stall gate.

"Clearing my head. Do you mind if I ride Brutus?" He asked.

"Sure, you're about the only one who can ride him." Trace nodded while brushing the colt down.

"I could help you with that." He offered.

"I've got Nutmeg and Cinnamon to ride." Trace declined.

"Are you getting many calls for stud fees?" He asked, leading the stallion out of his stall.

"Yes, things really picked up when he beat Artie's best horse. He wanted to buy him from me." Trace smirked. "As if."

"I'll be back in a little while." Shadow hopped on the horse's bare back and rode it out of the barn. When he cleared the fence line, he kicked the animal into a gallop and became one with the beast.

Cool wind whipped his long hair behind him as the magnificent horse flew across the pasture toward the mountain behind the ranch.

Shadow set his mind free as the call of his ancestors pulled him into the past. He could see the teepees in the distance near the creek that ran through the property. Children chased each other happily while the women tanned hides and cooked.

Warriors rode into camp with the bounty they'd killed on their hunt. The women began their work without wasting any part of the animals, while the men sharpened their arrowheads and mended bows and arrows.

The scene playing in his head seemed so real he could almost smell the smoke from the fires his ancestors tended. When Brutus snorted and reared back almost dumping him on the ground, he saw the fire racing toward them.

He allowed the horse to flee back to the barn. Leaning down over the horse he kicked it to go faster.

Trace looked up when Shadow slowed the horse and noticed the smoke in the distance.

"Trace! There's a fire by the creek!" He shouted sliding off the animal and turning him loose in the corral to cool down.

"I'll call Will, meet me at the truck!" Trace ran to the house.

Will showed up with his tractor and disk shortly after Trace and Shadow began beating the flames with wet cloths. He began making a fire break between the homestead and the creek. By the time, the fire was out every neighbor in the area had arrived to help, with huge tanks of water in their truck beds.

"I wonder what started it." Trace looked at Shadow.

"I don't know. I was daydreaming and Brutus alerted me. I high tailed it back to let you know." Shadow told him.

"Let's have a look see." Will said as Josh pulled up.

"Is it out?" Josh asked looking around.

"There's a few hot spots but for the most part it's out." Trace said.

The men fanned out to douse the hot spots until they reached the origin of the fire.

"Somebody set this." Josh said looking at the empty gasoline container.

"I'll bet it has something to do with that guy that has Elysa." Shadow growled. If he'd have known for sure the man was this close, he would've gotten her out of his clutches.

Will swore when Shadow made the comment. He got onto the tractor and drove as fast as he could back home hoping the feeling, he had was wrong.

Chapter Eleven

Marty waited until Will drove the tractor away from the ranch to help put out the fire he'd started. Sweat rolled down his back as he remembered how close that man had come to catching him. He wanted to make the fire much bigger, but the man had interrupted.

Quickly leaving his hiding place, he hurried to the back door of the house. He thought this was too easy when he found the door standing open. Slipping inside, he followed the sound of the woman singing. A snort left his mouth when he quietly made his way upstairs.

Anticipation filled him with each step toward the room the woman moved around in. He stopped leaning against the wall just outside the door.

***

Samantha ran a brush through her blond hair now streaked with silver gray strands. Sadness fell on her when she thought of her mother's passing shortly after her father had succumbed to cancer. There was so much time forever lost when their family ran from the stalker targeting her.

Now she cherished the good memories of the last few years. Thanks to her husband and his best friend, that threat was in the past never to happen again.

She slipped her shoes on to go meet her two children at the bus stop while Devlin slept and stepped out of her room unaware of the intruder waiting for her.

Marty grabbed the woman and shoved the chloroformed cloth in her face. The struggle didn't last long, and he hoisted her over his shoulder and hurried outside. He grabbed her purse and retrieved the keys to her SUV. After dumping her in the back, he slid behind the wheel and spewed gravel and dirt as he barreled out of the drive. In the rear-view mirror he saw the tractor with Will on it on the other side of the pasture.

The evil smile that formed on his lips. Revenge filled his heart as he thought about how distraught Will would be. He was the culprit that got him kicked out of the military. Frank went along for the ride in framing him.

He slid to a stop next to his SUV and transferred Will's wife into it and drove away with no one the wiser. The two women would be the ultimate price his old teammates would pay for what they had done.

***

Will jumped off the tractor and ran inside calling Samantha's name. He knew when he saw her car drive away that she wasn't there. It was more than obvious she hadn't left on her own when he saw her purse strewn about on the counter. The back door was standing wide open. She'd always insisted they lock the door if they weren't home.

The sound of boots in the kitchen drew him back downstairs after he checked the rooms for her and found Dev sleeping soundly in his bed.

"Will? What's going on?" Josh asked as Shadow and Trace followed.

"Samantha's been taken." Will growled slamming his fist into the wall.

"Are you sure?" Trace asked.

"The only thing missing from her purse is the keys to the SUV. She wouldn't leave her driver's license here." He related what he observed. "I saw the SUV drive away before I could get here."

"We'll find her." Josh assured him. "I'm going to head toward town so I can get a bolo out for her SUV."

When the bus let his children off, Will asked Spencer to watch his siblings before he slipped into his truck to visit Frank. Out of everyone, he knew Frank understood how he felt. He parked next to Frank's truck and sat for a minute to gather his thoughts and calm his heart. Samantha needed him now more than ever.

Frank met him at the door, "Come on in. Trace called to let us know what happened.

"We need to find Marty and put him in the ground." Will growled.

"If it were only that easy, but we have to do it by the book." Frank said.

"I know, but I can dream, can't I?" Will dropped down on the sofa.

"Who's watching the kids?" Ginger inquired as she put her girls in the playpen while the boys played with Legos on the floor next to them.

"Spencer is watching them for now. I really should get back." Will stood to leave.

"If you need anything, just let me know." Ginger hugged him.

"Thanks, I will." He moved toward the door.

"We'll find her. I'm sure Durango took her." Frank clapped his back.

"I'm torn on how to feel. If Durango's got her, I know it wasn't someone else. If it isn't, who?" He asked.

"Don't worry, I pr…" Frank began.

"Don't promise. Just help me find her." He shook his head.

"Already on it." Frank said, following him out of the house.

"I'll call later. See ya." Will said climbing into his truck.

The short drive across the road didn't give him enough time to cool down. When the door opened, Spencer stepped onto the porch and Will knew he had to tell him the truth.

Spencer was quickly becoming a young man. To say he was proud of his child was an understatement. Not that he took all the credit for how well his child turned out, he knew Samantha had the biggest hand in his raising.

"Dad? What's going on? Where's Mom?" Spencer asked with worry furrowing his brows.

"Someone took her. Uncle Frank and Uncle Josh are looking for her." Will explained.

"Will she be, okay?" He asked holding back tears while his jaw twitched.

"I don't know. We have to pray that God will protect her and Aunt Elysa." Will said honestly.

"I will. I promise." Spencer shoved his hands in his pockets.

"I know you will son. Don't tell Suzy she's too young to understand." Will pulled him in for a hug. "For now, come help me make dinner."

"I'll cook, you burn everything." Spencer snorted hugging his father back.

"I know, your mother says I can burn boiled water." Will chuckled.

"Let's go." Spencer moved toward the door praying in his heart that his mother was okay.

Chapter Twelve

Elysa jumped when the doors to the root cellar flew open. Temporarily blinded by the bright sunlight streaming across the cellar. His big bulky shadow crept along the floor as he made his way inside carrying someone over his shoulder like a sack of potatoes.

She watched him dump her on the other mat and turn to leave. After the cellar doors closed, she heard the heavy chain move and the lock click into place.

Cautiously stepping toward the unconscious woman, she recognized the sundress she'd given Samantha. Dropping to her knees, she carefully turned the woman onto her back.

There was no doubt in her mind Marty had drugged her. She had been around the woman enough to know she wouldn't go down without a fight. Elysa shook her lightly hoping she would awaken soon. After her month-long captivity she craved company. Now she knew what it felt like to be in solitary confinement, except the conditions might be just slightly better in prison.

Samantha slowly regained consciousness. Confusion held her for a moment when her eyes focused on the young woman sitting beside her. "Elysa?"

"Samantha? Are you okay?" He didn't hurt you, did he?" Elysa spouted questions like old faithful.

"I think so. At least I don't hurt anywhere." She struggled to sit up but decided against it when the room swam before her.

"Give yourself a few minutes for the drug to wear off." Elysa insisted.

"Do you have any water?" She asked with a dry throat.

"No, he only gives me a small bottle of water with my meals." Elysa shook her head.

"How long have you been here?" She looked around the dirt cellar.

"I think somewhere around a month. They took me when I was in Denver and brought me here." Elysa said.

"Who is they?" She asked, confused.

"Marty and his twin brother Paul. Marty's not so bad, but Paul is a pure-bred psycho." Elysa told her.

"He didn't..." She couldn't say the words.

"No. He did however beat me for complaining about the accommodations. I learned really quick that Paul would lose it if you challenged him." Elysa rubbed her cheek where he'd struck her for asking him to dump the bucket, she used to relieve herself.

"We need to get outta here." She sat up slowly.

"I've tried but there's only one way in or out." Elysa pointed at the door. "There's nothing to defend ourselves either. The only things here are our mats and that bucket to use if you need to relieve yourself."

"How utterly nice of them." She grimaced.

"Just keep your mouth shut around Paul and if he asks you a question answer with the bare minimum of words. He has no patience at all. Marty feeds me, us now, twice a day. It isn't great, but it fills the hole for a little bit." Elysa warned her.

"We should look for any opening we can to get outta here." She said emphatically.

***

Marty sat down with a glass of cold ice water as fatigue gnawed at him. Paul kept pushing the boundaries he had set up. The more he did, the stronger he became. Marty knew his strength to fight his brother faded with each line Paul crossed. One day he realized Paul would have no more use for him and he'd disappear into the vast wasteland of memories.

"Did you get the camera?" Paul interrupted his thoughts.

"Yes, I'll take their pictures when I give them dinner." Marty replied.

"No. I'll do it. I'm going to give Bear and Wolf a little memento to prove I have them." Paul grinned.

"What are you gonna do?" Marty panicked.

"You don't worry about that; I'll see to them. You just get their food ready." Paul ordered.

Marty knew if he didn't the headache his brother gave him would intensify enough; he'd have to retire early for bed. He put the plain bologna and cheese sandwiches in the lunch box with two small bottles of water.

"Are you done?" Paul asked, grabbing the camera.

"Yes." Marty held the lunch box up.

"Good, now for a little fun." Paul's face transformed into the face of pure evil.

Marty went along for the ride not that he had any choice. At least he could try to protect the two women from any lasting damage his brother was capable of inflicting on them.

***

Samantha and Elysa huddled together in the corner on the mat Marty had dumped her on. The sound of the lock opening, and the chain rattling sent the fear of the unknown racing through the women.

The light from the sunset flooded the darkness as the bulky form of their captor threw the door open. His shadow grew closer to them with each menacing step he took.

"Don't get any ideas of escaping, you won't survive it." Paul growled when he saw them.

"Here's your dinner." Paul set the lunchbox down near them.

"Look up and smile for the camera." Paul held the camera up and snapped pictures of them. Then he advanced on them with a long knife with jagged edges.

Terror filled the women when he reached for Samantha's long hair and cut a huge hunk from her head. Then he turned to Elysa and did the same.

"Why are you cutting our hair?" Samantha asked just before she felt the slap across her face. Instinctively she knew not to move or show emotion.

"Keep your mouth shut and worry about how long I let you live." Paul snarled as he turned to leave.

They stared at Paul's retreating back leaving darkness in his wake. After the lock clicked Elysa peered into the darkness barely making out Samantha's form.

"Are you okay?" She asked.

"Yeah. I shouldn't have asked." Samantha rubbed her bruised cheek.

"You got off easy. The first time I said anything he didn't like; he beat me up." She divulged.

"Will and Frank will find us." Samantha told her, trying to hang onto the hope they were looking for her. "Frank, Shadow and Hawk have been looking for you for several weeks now."

"Did they find my luggage and camera equipment?" She asked hopefully.

"I believe so. They've hit a brick wall looking for you. But I refuse to believe they won't find us." Samantha said confidently.

"If I know my brother, he'll move heaven and earth to find me and so will Wolfie." She replied before handing Samantha a sandwich and the tiny bottle of water before nibbling on hers.

Chapter Thirteen

Shadow, Hawk, Will and Frank sat in the conference room at the Wolf Creek Police Station waiting for Josh to bring the file he had on Samantha and Elysa's disappearance. The men looked up when Josh came into the room.

"Did you find them?" Will asked hopefully.

"I found her SUV parked off the road a mile away from your house. Samantha and her captor were long gone. I'll drive you out there so you can take it home." Josh said.

"Were there any other clues left behind." Will asked.

"He either wore gloves or wiped everything down because there weren't any fingerprints. It looks as though he threw Samantha in the back because I found one of her shoes on the ground beneath the back bumper." Josh told them. "I don't have anything else to go on. I'm not giving up, but at this point, well…" Josh shoved his fingers through his hair.

"I know you're doing everything you can to find them." Will sighed, doing his best not to lose hope.

"I'm going to the office in Sheridan, Abe might have something." Frank said moving to get up.

Josh followed the men out while Will picked up the baby carrier little Dev sat in playing with the toys secured at the handle. Josh stopped to allow his brother to move past him.

"I'll do my best to find her. I'm gonna talk to Joe and Kevin about it for any ideas." Josh promised.

"I know you will. Tell Jillian I said hi." Will sighed as he left the building.

***

Ginger paced the floor with a fussy little Amanda. She knew the baby's gums were swollen from her tiny teeth pushing to get through. When she felt the child's breath even out, she put her in the playpen. Thankfully, the other three were in bed.

Frank walked in feeling defeated. If only they had a clue to where his sister and Samantha were. He had no doubt Marty Durango held them hostage. Now more than ever he feared for their safety. In the service the man acted normal until a mission came up for them then he changed into a man obsessed with killing. At times he thought Marty lived just on the edge of morality and depravity.

Ginger touched his arm drawing him from his thoughts. He didn't know she was there, and he jerked his fist back before it connected to her jaw. "I'm so sorry!"

"Since you didn't hit me, and I know where your mind is, I'll let it slide." She said handing him the bundle of that day's mail. "You'll get a break and find them both."

He set the mail on the table next to the hat rack and pulled her in for a long kiss. His wife and kids were his world and he loved them dearly.

***

Will sat down in his office to open the mail while Spencer entertained Suzy and Dev. One after another he opened the envelopes until he came to one with no postmark and Wolf written in large letters where the address should've been.

Carefully opening it, a large swatch of Samantha's hair fell on the desk when he pulled the note out. It read:

"Wolf. It's been a long time since they put me into the brig. I lost everything because of you and Bear. I mostly blame you for my imprisonment. Frank only followed your orders, of course so did Dev and Omar.

59

They acted like little puppies following their mother around.

You don't know how angry we became when you left us out of your little Charlie Foxtrot club. Too bad you didn't see how sick it made the rest of us when you four pranced around like little gods in front of us.

Now the tables have turned. We hold all the cards and if you wanna see your wife again you'll do exactly as I say from here on out. Make no mistake, you fail in any way and your luscious wife will know what the word sadistic means. I'll make sure to document everything, so you won't miss out on the fun.

I've been watching you and Bear for months now. I know you ain't rich like Frank is, but I'm sure if you get on your knees and beg, he'll pay for your wife's freedom as well as his sister's life.

I'll contact you later when I decide what I really want from you.

M"

Will grabbed his phone and dialed Frank's number.

***

Ginger wrapped her arms around her husband. He hid his worry, but she could tell. She was worried too. The phone rang, interrupting them. Reluctantly, Frank went into his office to answer the phone.

'Hello?" He answered sitting in his chair.

"Bear, it's Wolf. Did you get a letter from Marty today?" Will asked.

"I haven't looked yet, hang on." He said rushing to get the mail from the table. Grabbing the stack, he hurried back to his office.

It took only a second to find the envelope with only his name on it. Ripping it opened a swatch of Elysa's dark hair fell out. He read the letter to his friend getting angrier with each word.

"It's identical to the one he sent me with Samantha's hair in it." Will sighed.

"You don't worry about the money if he asks for it, and you don't have it. I can sell my extra shares in CFS and sell some stocks. I can have it together in twenty-four hours. We'll get the girls back." Frank insisted.

"I can't ask you to do that Bear! I'll figure something out when the time comes." Will declined. "Besides, he may want something other than money."

"Wolf, you're my family and I'll do anything for family. Now let me alert the bank and the stockholders of what may happen, we'll take care of it in the morning." Frank insisted.

"I'll literally be forever in your debt." Will managed around the watermelon that planted itself in his throat.

"So, when you win the lottery, you can pay me back." Frank tried to ease his friend's emotional state.

"You gotta play to win. I don't but I'll start." Will tried to sound happy, but Frank knew better.

"I'll pick you up in the morning. Sleep if you can." Frank said.

"Yeah right. See you tomorrow." Will sighed as he ended the call.

Chapter Fourteen

Shadow sat at his sister's table while Trace fed little Allen. A large smile formed on his lips when Allen spit the food in Trace's face.

"What's so funny?" Trace glowered at him while wiping the pureed food off.

"Not a thing." Shadow chuckled as Trace tried another bite of the food.

"I can't blame you buddy; I wouldn't eat this stuff either." Track told his son as he spit it out again. "Star! Get him something else to eat, he don't like this pureed lima bean. Who eats lima beans for breakfast anyhow? I wouldn't touch them with a ten-foot pole."

"Let me try." Shadow offered.

"Be my guest." Trace stood and handed him the warm food.

"Okay." Shadow sat in the chair. "You are going to be a strong brave one day and you must eat all your food no matter what it is."

Trace watched with rapt attention of the interaction between his brother-in-law and son. His mouth dropped open when the little tyke ate every bite before Shadow gave him applesauce to round out his meal.

"How did you do that?" Trace asked suspiciously.

"You lose your cool to easy and he knows you don't like the food, so he reacts accordingly." Shadow explained.

"Then from now on, you get to feed him the lima beans." Trace grumbled.

Shadow snorted when Star kissed her husband on the cheek. "I'm going to Frank's. I hope something has come up, but since he hasn't called me, I'm not waiting around on him."

"You will find them my brother." Star said in Lakota.

Trace understood the conversation since Star had instructed him in their language.

"Come back for dinner tonight." Star insisted.

"Depends upon what happens today." Shadow said moving to leave. "I'll be here unless we get a lead."

Star kissed his cheek and hugged him before he left. Shadow wished Elysa had been the one to kiss him instead of his sister. He got into his truck and saw Frank's truck parked in Will's driveway, so he drove to his house just as Frank backed up to turn around.

Shadow parked and jumped out when Frank stopped upon seeing him.

"Where are you going?" Shadow asked.

Frank told him to get in and he would explain everything.

He settled in the back seat of the king cab next to Dev. After Frank told him about the events from the night before, he kept little Dev occupied. The little tyke giggled when Shadow tickled his little toes.

Even though he enjoyed the little ones around him, Shadow wanted his own babies. Deep down he prayed Elysa would be his wife and the mother of his children. If only he could get a solid lead on her whereabouts, he'd get Hawk and Kevin and deal with this Durango character the Lakota way. He would pay for treating Elysa and Samantha so roughly.

Frank parked in his reserved slot in the garage. The men rode the small elevator to the floor CFS occupied. They split up when they exited the elevator. Frank and Will went to his office to begin the process of getting the two million together.

Shadow found Hawk coming out of the small breakroom on his way to Abe's cave.

"What's up?" Hawk asked, following him down the hall.

"I want to find out if Abe has made any progress in nailing down Elysa and Samantha's whereabouts." He said as they reached the bat cave.

"Anything?" Shadow asked hoping he had something.

"I sure do. That little diner across from the motel Elysa checked into had security cameras. I caught the SUV driving out of the parking lot. Durango was driving and I got the tag number." Abe put the video on the screen behind him. "It's taking me a while to track him through Denver. I lost him when he got on interstate twenty-five. On the upside, he headed north, so I'd be willing to bet he's headed toward Wolf Creek."

"Can you contact the state police to see if they'll be on the lookout for the SUV?" Shadow asked.

"Already done, but no one has seen him yet. All we can do is pray this guy makes a mistake." Abe replied still typing. "I'll let Frank know when I hear something."

Shadow and Hawk left the room and went to Frank's office to see how things were going with them.

"I'll have to go to the bank to finalize everything when we know more." Frank stood up. The shares in the company brought almost a third of the money. The main investors, his friends from the military including Hawk, were happy to buy another share each. Now he had to rearrange his investments and sell off other stocks he knew would make up the rest.

Will stood up when Hawk and Shadow appeared in the doorway. "Any news?"

Shadow explained what Abe told him. "He'll let you know Frank if anything turns up."

"We're heading to the bank, I want y'all to follow us should anything happen I want backup in case Marty is watching" Frank insisted.

Chapter Fifteen

Elysa and Samantha huddled in the corner shaking in terror. During the afternoon, a rattlesnake found its way into the cellar. Too terrified to move, the slimy thing slithered along the wall toward them.

"What do we do?" Elysa shuddered.

"Don't move and hope it leaves." Samantha whispered.

The cellar door moved a tiny bit when the lock snapped open, and the chain fell away. Marty moved inside unaware of the danger lurking between him and the women.

"What's wrong?" He asked moving toward them as the reptile coiled and shook its tail in warning.

Before he could move the snake sunk its teeth into Marty's pant leg. Thankfully, he wore boots, so it didn't hurt him, but the gunshot from the pistol he carried deafened everyone as the snake wiggled in death throes.

Marty picked it up and chunked it out of the cellar before returning with their food for the night.

"We can't stay here if snakes are gonna start visiting. It's bad enough that spiders and other critters are crawling around." Samantha said knowing she'd pay for it.

The punch he threw at her brought stars to her vision.

"You'll stay here and behave or else." Paul growled.

The brothers were identical right down to their clothes, so they never knew which one was dealing with them until Paul lashed out. Marty hadn't actually hit them, but he did drug them.

Samantha rubbed her cheek as Paul left them. After he chained and locked the door, she looked at Elysa.

"I think Marty and Paul are the same person." She observed.

"I thought so too, but I don't know. Their personalities are so different." Elysa agreed.

"I knew the man was unstable, but if he has a split personality, we may be in more trouble than we know." She commented.

"I have noticed Marty doesn't carry a gun so maybe they are twins after all." Elysa added hoping Samantha was wrong.

"We'll find out eventually." She said opening the lunch box to the same kind of sandwiches and little eight-ounce water bottles.

Without another word they choked down the bread and meat and drank the water wondering how long they would hold them captive.

Marty sat down on the well-worn couch in the small house they hid out in.

"It's time to stir up some trouble in Wolf Creek." Paul cut into his thoughts.

"No. Those people haven't done anything to us. We're only after Wolf and Bear." Marty shook his head.

"You have always been weak. Even in the service I had to be the brave one." Paul snarled.

"I know you kept me safe back then, but this is different. Those people aren't terrorists or kidnappers." Marty felt another headache pushing its way into his mind.

"Go lay down. You'll feel better after you rest." Paul insisted.

"What do you have planned?" Marty asked suspiciously.

"Nothing. You need to sleep, I'll keep watch." Paul shook his head innocently.

Marty gave in and laid down after taking more painkillers. His headaches grew progressively worse the more Paul argued with him, and that was a problem.

One day he knew deep down in the depths of his soul, Paul would take over and leave him behind.

His brother grew in strength each day and Marty could feel himself slipping a little more. He closed his eyes drifting into a deep sleep.

Paul had other plans. As soon as Marty dozed, he was outside getting into the SUV. He yanked the cover off the hidden compartment in the back. His fingers touched the rifle he chose to use, he grabbed it and the ammo he needed. Sliding behind the wheel, he backed up and drove toward Wolf Creek. What Marty didn't know wouldn't hurt him.

***

Hoss finished with the broken wire on the fence. This was the fourth one today that someone had cut. The person chose the furthest fence to sabotage from the house. Frustrated, he threw the old wire in the back of his truck along with his other equipment. He started to open the door to get into the cab when a shot rang out. White hot pain shot through his shoulder and another shot sounded when a bullet hit his leg.

He managed to dive into the truck and drive it away with shots firing from behind. Thankfully, the person quit firing after he got out of range. Stars danced before his eyes as he fought to stay conscious. He drove to Trace's house because he knew Star could help him.

Trace looked up when he heard the truck slowing down as it neared the pasture gate. When it drove through it, Trace ran toward the advancing vehicle. He managed to jump in the passenger side of the truck and cut the engine as it rolled to a stop.

"Hoss!" Trace shouted to wake him as he saw his blood-soaked shirt and jeans.

"Star!" He shouted. "Call the nine-one-one dispatcher. Get Josh and an ambulance out here!"

While she disappeared inside, he struggled to get the behemoth man from the truck and on the ground. As he put pressure on the wounds, he heard the shot ring out just before it hit him in the shoulder.

"Trace!" Star screamed as she started for him.

"Stay in the house!" Trace yelled as another shot hit the ground in front of Star. She immediately ran back inside.

Trace kept applying pressure to Hoss' leg, but his shoulder injury prevented him from doing the same to the man's shoulder.

Another shot rang out barely missing him. He got the distinct impression the man missed on purpose. Nevertheless, he had to get them out of the line of fire. With all the strength he could gather, he managed to get them both to safety. The sounds of sirens reached his ears just as everything went black.

***

Ginger put the last of her children down for a nap when she heard gunfire. Rushing downstairs, she grabbed her trusty shotgun and slipped out of the front door to find her brother Jarod on the ground with blood pouring from his shoulder.

The moment she took a step toward her brother, another shot rang out and she saw the direction it came from. Raising her shotgun, she fired both barrels in the general direction.

Hoping the sniper had left when she fired, she managed to get Jarod inside just as another round hit the window beside her. She quickly shoved her brother into the house and closed the door behind her.

She called the dispatch and Kelly informed her they would be there as soon as possible.

Jarod moaned as blood pooled around his shoulder. Ginger ran to the kitchen and grabbed the first aid kit Frank had stocked there and hurried back to bandage up

the wound until the ambulance arrived for him. She
didn't know what happened at Trace's home.

Chapter Sixteen

Paul drove back toward the town of Wolf Creek ready to wreak more havoc while their small police force dealt with the mayhem he'd caused at the ranches. Parking in an abandoned drive hidden from the main road, he hiked back to the south end of town. After picking the perfect tree, he climbed into its thick foliage and looked through his scope to find the peaceful small town going about its business without a care in the world.

Larry walked Ms. Gunn back to the courthouse after lunch. He couldn't believe the woman actually liked him. He was a bartender and owner. In his view he wasn't good enough for her, but who was he to complain?

He heard the shot before Charlotte crumpled to the ground screaming as blood stained the shoulder of her dress.

"I gotta get you outta here." Larry tried to help her up when a searing pain hit his leg after another shot rang out.

Together they crawled behind the mailbox on the street. They watched in horror as people running in panic fell to the ground screaming in pain. Larry felt helpless watching the citizens of Wolf Creek scurry for cover while others cried out for help.

As quickly as the attack started, it ended. Larry watched the only ambulance they had pull into the emergency room as the few medical personnel poured out of the hospital to help those on the street. The EMT's pulled a stretcher out and rushed inside, then returned with two more gurneys to unload two more patients.

When he saw them help his brother and Trace onto the beds, he wondered why anyone would shoot so many people. What had the town done to make someone do such damage?

"It's gonna be okay, Charlotte." Larry tried to soothe her while fighting the darkness gathering at the edge of his vision.

Josh pulled up to the curb when he saw the carnage in the streets. One by one, he helped the injured into the bed of his truck while James did the same. When they got to Larry, Charlotte had passed out from the pain, and he could barely keep his wits about him.

"It's gonna be okay bro." James said picking up Charlotte and then returning to help him into the truck.

After the injured were in the ER, Josh grabbed his cell and called Will.

"Hey, what's going on?" Will answered.

"Where are y'all? We gotta big problem. Someone shot Trace and Hoss. Then shot Jarod. When we got to town fifteen people lay in the street with bullet wounds. They shot Larry and Charlotte too." Josh growled angrily.

"We're on our way." Will said ending the call.

"What's up?" Frank asked after talking with the bank manager.

"Somebody shot up our ranches and the town. Josh said around twenty people are suffering from gunshot wounds." Will said, moving toward the door of the bank with Frank following swearing under his breath.

Shadow and Hawk saw the two men exit the bank and could tell something had happened.

"Follow us to Wolf Creek! Somebody shot up the town and our ranches!" Frank yelled as they got into his truck.

Josh directed traffic as word spread fast through the community. He'd much rather be inside with his family, but he had to help out with the onslaught of cars and trucks racing to find out if their loved ones would survive. Of course, there were always looky-loos itching to see what happened. James faced the same circumstances even though he worked on the other side of the town.

Doc had called the hospital in Sheridan to ask for both ambulance and air lift support. Not only did they have life-threatening injuries, but they didn't have enough beds for everyone.

When Frank and Will arrived, they helped where needed. The men helped the nurses lifting the victims onto gurneys or into wheelchairs. The nursing staff felt relieved when they pitched in.

Like most little towns, they never imagined something of this magnitude and evil would take place in their hometown. That meant there wasn't a plan in place to care for the scale of injuries the sniper inflicted on the townsfolk.

When the last ambulance left for Sheridan, Josh met James and Joe in the waiting room with their families.

"How are Trace and Jarod?" Josh asked.

"They'll make it. Hoss suffered from two wounds and lost a lot of blood, but he'll recover. He's gonna be down for a few weeks as well as Trace." Ginger explained rocking the two strollers to keep the babies quiet.

"How about Larry and Charlotte?" James asked.

"Larry's leg broke when the bullet lodged against it. Charlotte will have to take some time off with a broken collarbone." Joe replied.

"How many died?" Josh swallowed. He knew everyone in town. They were family in his book.

"Sadie Walsh from a gunshot wound, Ethel Davis suffered a heart attack trying to help Sadie, and Mary Watsons, the town treasurer. Everyone else suffered from either a bullet wound or scrapes and bruises while trying to find cover." Joe said with mixed emotions that switched from sorrow to anger and back again.

"Did you find out where the sniper was?" Frank asked.

"As near as I can tell the assault came from the south end of town. I couldn't really see much since I was helping the injured out of the street." Joe growled. "What I can't figure out is why anyone would just randomly take pot shots at anything that moved. Shoot the guy even shot the dog and cat Sadie and Ethel owned."

"We might know the answer to that." Will spoke up knowing Joe was going to kick their tails.

"Who?" Joe asked, growing even more angry.

Frank explained everything. Joe already knew Elysa and Samantha were missing, but he didn't know why or who took them. When Frank finished his voice trailed off when Joe, red face mad opened his mouth.

"When were you gonna tell me about this? After you've found them?" He yelled drawing the attention of everyone seated in the waiting room.

"I didn't think about telling you because I had everything under control." Frank replied withering from the look Joe sent him.

"I'm at fault too Joe. We're so wrapped up looking for the girls I didn't think to tell you." Will said unwilling to let Frank take all the blame.

"Let me tell you something boys. I'm the law in this town and nobody has the right to circumvent my authority. I get that you're the best in the security business, but you have no authority to do anything unless I okay it." Joe exploded. "From now on, you come to me with anything that requires an investigation concerning any of our residents. You boys are good men, but you have a habit of going off on your own. If

it happens again, you'll see the inside of the jail for a
few days."

Joe, finished with his rant, stomped from the room to
see if any of the victims could talk to him.

"Wow, I ain't never seen Joe so angry at anyone.
Not even when he caught us having that beer party out
by the creek when we were younger." Josh said happy
he wasn't in his boss' crosshairs.

Chapter Seventeen

Marty sat up feeling something wasn't right. He looked around the room and found his long-range snipers rifle lying across the table.

"What did you do Paul?" He growled.

"I put some fear into that little town." Paul chuckled. "You should have seen them running around like rats in a maze looking for cover."

"Why would you do that? Those people have done nothing to us!" Marty shouted.

"The accepted Wolf and Bear into their community. They're all just like them. You don't think for a minute if they catch us, we'll wind up in a prison or worse lynched on one of their ranches?" Paul argued.

"You've got to stop doing things while I'm resting. You'll make a mistake, and they will catch us." Marty growled. "We need to stick to our plan, so stop deviating from it."

"You know one of these days I'll gain control over you, and you'll wind up a foot note in someone's journal. Don't cross me, Marty. I'm warning you." Paul threatened him.

"I'm gonna go feed the women. And while I'm thinking about it, leave them alone. They are innocent in all this." Marty grabbed the lunch box from the cooler.

"The whole reason we took them was to make Wolf and Bear pay for what they did to us." Paul growled. "I plan to execute them while their loved one's watch."

"No! We get the money and let them go." Marty insisted.

"We'll see dear brother, we'll see." Paul said. "I'm tired so I think I'll sleep for a while."

Marty sighed as the headache his brother consistently brought eased. He finally delivered the women's food and locked the door before going for a few supplies.

His brother's actions only added to the immense stress on his shoulders. Did anyone see his brother while he shot up the town? They needed to end this soon or he feared his brother's threat of overriding his decisions would become a reality.

Shadow, Kevin, and Hawk helped Will, Frank, and Joe track the sniper. The trail ended when they found the SUV tracks leaving the place the man had hidden it.

"Looks like he got away." Joe sighed angrily.

"I'm sure we'll catch the guy eventually." Hawk reassured him.

"I'm still angry at y'all for keeping me in the dark about Samantha and Elysa. If I had known, we could have avoided all the townsfolk being shot at." Joe growled.

"It slipped their minds because they're used to doing things on their own. How long have you known Will? I'll wager since he was in kindergarten." Hawk said. "The time we spent in the military not only did they hone the independent side of us, but it also taught us to work as a team. They made an honest mistake and I'm sure they regret it."

"It's too late for apologies and excuses now. I have a town to protect and y'all better keep me informed." Joe settled his eyes on each one of them.

"I'll make sure of it, Joe. We truly didn't mean to keep you out of the loop." Frank promised.

"See that it doesn't happen again." Joe walked away.

Kevin and Shadow found the tree the sniper fired on the town from and collected the empty shell casings.

"Here's the shells we gathered but there's not much else. The man was careful to hide his tracks." Hawk handed the shells to Joe.

"Frank, aren't these military grade shells?" Joe held them out to him.

"They sure are. We're dealing with Durango, and he has contacts to buy them." Frank's inside shook with anger. "I need to tell you something else. Don't underestimate him. Like me he's a trained killer but, he's gone bad. He won't hesitate to use every single second of his training against you."

"Why is he out for you and Will?" Joe asked, realizing he didn't know the entire story.

Frank came clean with every detail he could without breaking the confidentiality of the military as he rode back to town with Joe.

The longer Joe listened the more his emotions churned inside of him. Not only did he disapprove of leaving him in the dark, but his anger at the psychopath who shot up the town posed more of a danger than he knew Wolf Creek was prepared for.

He stopped at the hospital to talk to the injured. Trace gave Joe his statement describing the incident at their ranch. Then Joe went to Jarod's room and found the same story of the shot coming from a distance.

Disheartened, he left the hospital to create the reports and begin an in-depth investigation into the shootings. Not once in his forty-five years as sheriff had anything like this ever happened.

He worked long into the night going over other witness statements, looking for next of kin for those who didn't survive their injuries.

The next morning still blurry eyed from little to no sleep, Joe pulled the death certificates for Ethel and Sadie, as a sad smile crossed his face. How many times over the years had he climbed that stupid tree to retrieve the terrified cat?

At first, he didn't mind, but the older the two ladies became, the more they fought. Thinking back on it he realized they didn't have any family come by for a visit, so they became sisters that weren't happy unless they were bickering at each other.

He closed the file saddened that the two women had no one left in their families. Someone would have to clean their houses out and look for a will or anything stating a beneficiary.

The next file for Mary Watkins fell open on the desk. Her next of kin lived on a ranch south of Wolf Creek. With a sad sigh, he grabbed his hat and headed for the front door. He always hated to be the bearer of sad news. Even after all these years it never got any easier.

"Kelly, I'm going to the Watkins' ranch. I don't know how long I'll be there." He informed his dispatch/receptionist.

"I'll say a prayer for them." She looked up with tears in her eyes. "Why would someone shoot innocent people for no reason?"

"That's a question only time will tell. There are evil people in this world, but I choose to believe that God has many more good people out there that make up for the bad." He answered and left praying for wisdom when he reached the ranch.

Chapter Eighteen

Marty parked the new truck he found. Even though his brother would throw a fit, he knew that sticking with the same vehicle for too long would draw attention. There is no telling who might write down a tag number or see something they felt uneasy about when they drove by.

His brother had the decency to wait until he put the tiny bit of food and water on the counter before he started in on him. "Where have you been? What did you do with the SUV? Where did you get the truck?"

"I went for more food and water; I traded the SUV in on that truck. We've had it too long and I don't want anyone to track us." Marty sighed as the usual headache began growing the longer his brother ranted. "I need to feed the women, then I'm going to sleep."

"I'll feed them and take some pictures of them to send along. It's about time to contact their families again." He growled while grabbing the camera and heading out of the door.

Marty knew when he left the dilapidated cabin that his brother wouldn't hold back his fury. Even in their youth, Paul often tried to push his will on him. His brother had a sadistic streak in him and used it at every opportunity they found themselves in. Back when they were younger, Marty was able to control him with ease. Now, his fears were coming true little by little. Quite frankly, Marty grew tired of fighting for the dominance he once had a firm hold on.

Samantha couldn't take anymore bologna. She never liked the stuff to begin with. When Paul gave the food to them, she grumbled under her breath wishing for something else.

She never saw the blow coming until his fist connected with her face. The man took his anger out on her instead of his brother. When Elysa stepped in to keep him from killing her, she landed in a heap against the dirt wall. In his rage, he turned on her until Marty yelled at him to stop.

"You're killing them! If you want the revenge you seek, it won't happen if they're already dead."

Paul snapped out of his blind rage and stepped away from the women. He grabbed the camera and took the pictures, then left. Marty hurried back with the first aid kit he kept in the small shack.

When he returned both women sat huddled in the corner crying from the insurmountable pain Paul dished out to them.

"I'm sorry he hurt you so badly. This is the best I can do since we don't have ice." Marty handed them the two threadbare towels.

The women accepted the offering and held the lukewarm cloths to their faces. In that moment, their eyes met with the understanding they wouldn't come out of this alive.

"I'll be back in the morning with your breakfast." He left them alone in the darkness.

Samantha grabbed Elysa's hands and they prayed for God to guide their loved ones to them before the inevitable happened.

Marty stomped into the cabin holding his head. He found that when Paul gave into the bottomless pit of darkness he lived in, his headaches became almost unbearable.

"You didn't have to hurt them like that! All they want is something different to eat. Two months of dry bologna and cheese sandwiches would even make you sick!" Marty yelled at him.

"Calm down, I'm gonna go find another place closer to Wolf Creek and mail these pictures to Wolf and Bear." Paul snatched the envelopes off the small table.

"It would do you a world of good to take a nap while I'm gone."

Before Marty could answer Paul left the shack and drove away. What would he do now? The entire plan was beginning to fall apart because his brother couldn't control himself.

***

Joe drove away from Watkin's ranch relieved that was over. The family fell apart before his eyes. Although the children were in their teens, telling them their mother died from a sniper's bullet didn't give them much comfort. Their entire world changed in a blink of an eye.

He turned toward Wolf Creek as a blue pickup flew past him going way too fast. With a heavy sigh he flipped his lights on and radioed the license plate number, make and model of the truck. After telling Kelly where he was, he sped up to catch the man driving.

When the truck pulled over, Joe grabbed his ticket book and got out of his jeep. Cautiously he approached the vehicle, stopping just shy of the driver's side door.

Everything happened so fast Joe didn't know what hit him. A moment before falling unconscious on the ground, he looked down at his chest to see a small spot of blood grow rapidly surrounding the hole left by the bullet.

Paul got out and kicked Joe several times in the head and his torso. When his rage eased, he pulled the two envelopes out with the pictures in them and stuffed them in Joe's bloody shirt. With a little bit of blood on them Bear and Wolf would feel the helplessness his brother felt in the brig.

Paul turned toward the western side of Wolf Creek looking for another place to hide out until he could arrange things with his brother's old nemesis from their military days.

Chapter Nineteen

"Josh! I'm glad you're here. Joe stopped a speeding truck thirty minutes ago and I can't reach him." Kelly said as he walked into the station.

"Did he tell you where he was? Josh asked as James walked in behind him.

She gave him the location and the two men jumped in Josh's truck and sped to the last location Kelly had on him.

In no time they spotted Joe and his jeep. Josh skidded to a stop and hurried to help Joe while James called for an ambulance.

Before he started applying pressure to the wound, he pulled the two letters away from the bloody shirt. Without looking at them, he shoved them in his back pocket and went to work keeping his boss alive until the EMT's arrived.

After the ambulance left with Joe, the two men cleared the crime scene disappointed they hadn't found a clue to who had ambushed Joe.

Josh followed James, who drove Joe's jeep, back to the station. He sent James to the hospital while he called Frank and Will.

"Hello?" Will answered.

"Hey, it's Josh, I need you and Frank in my office, immediately." Josh told him.

"We'll be right there." Will understood Josh better than to waste time asking questions.

Josh dusted the envelopes for fingerprints but found only his. He wouldn't open them since they weren't his to open.

He looked up when Will and Frank stepped into his office.

"What's up?" Frank asked, eyeing the envelopes on his desk.

"Joe had a run in with someone and they shot him. When James and I found him, these were shoved in his shirt. He was unconscious and bleeding severely." Josh explained, handing them the envelopes. "I don't know his condition, but it doesn't look good. Whoever did this did a number on him."

They carefully opened the envelopes and swore when the pictures of their loved ones fell onto the desk. The bruises and bloody lips sent them into instant rage and fear for the girls.

"Durango." They both growled in unison.

"Did he include a ransom note or anything?" Josh asked.

"No, he's torturing us." Will growled.

"I'll go out on a limb and say he's the one who shot Joe." Frank said angrily.

"It's a good bet since he stuffed those into Joe's shirt. I need to get back over there to see how he's doing." Josh stood to leave. "Y'all keep me in the loop if you decide to do something."

"We will." They promised as they followed him out of the office.

***

Marty sat up on the worthless cot feeling worse than when he went to sleep. Deep down he had the sense his brother had been up to something while he slept.

"You need to get the women ready for a move. Go feed them then we can load them into the truck." Paul's voice cut into his thoughts.

"Where are we taking them?" Marty asked.

"I found a place west of Wolf Creek. It looks like an abandoned ranch." Paul answered.

"Any place is better than this one." Marty made the sandwiches for the women and left to feed them without knowing the water contained drugs to knock them out.

The sun seemed unusually bright when he stepped out of the shack. After unlocking the door to the root cellar, he went inside with the food.

They looked pitiful with the bruises on their faces. Even in pain, they managed to eat the dry sandwiches and drink the water.

Fifteen minutes later, they were sleeping soundly on the mats Marty insisted Paul give them.

"You drugged them?" Marty shouted.

"This way they won't wake up until well after we've arrived at the ranch." Paul shrugged.

"I went along with the chloroform but drugging them with any other drug wasn't part of the deal." Marty growled.

"It's too late to worry about it now. Let's get them in the truck and leave." Paul insisted.

"You need to remember who is in charge here! We do things my way!" Marty stomped toward the door.

"For now." Paul said and fell silent.

The one thing Marty feared in the last few years was Paul asserting himself and taking over everything. Somehow, he had managed to stop him. Paul was merciless and sadistic. His control over Paul weakened with every step they took in the revenge he sought.

Soon Marty put the two mats in the truck bed then laid the girls on them. To keep them out of sight, he put a tarp over them. Before long they were on their way to the ranch Paul had found when it occurred to him Paul hadn't confirmed he mailed the pictures to the objects of their what some people would call obsession.

When asked about it, Paul smirked. "I hand delivered it to the sheriff."

"What?" Marty asked in surprised shock.

"Don't worry, he's probably dead by now." Paul then explained what happened.

"You're taking too many chances! If you aren't careful, they'll catch us." Marty growled.

"No worries. That sheriff won't remember anything if he wakes up." Paul said.

"What makes you so sure?" Marty asked as his stomach tied in knots.

"I kicked him in the head hard enough to kill him, if he does survive, he'll have some kind of memory loss." Paul insisted. "Now turn left at the next driveway.

Marty followed his instructions and drove under the Anderson Ranch sign.

After taking the girls to the root cellar beneath the pantry, Marty parked the truck in the barn to keep it out of sight.

The excitement of finally getting his revenge changed to worry that Paul would get them caught. One thing Marty couldn't understand about his brother, why was he so adamant about taking over?

With a heavy sigh, he went back inside and figured out where they would sleep. He was happy to find some furnishings left behind by the owners. From the look of things, no one had set foot inside the house in a long time.

Chapter Twenty

Shadow empathized with Will. Even though he hadn't actually taken Elysa on a date yet, he knew what the man felt. In his estimation this entire thing was taking too long to resolve.

They should have found the women by now, or at the very least had clue about where they were. What bothered him the most was, from what he'd learned from Will, Frank, and Hawk, would the man let the girls live? Something in his gut said no. With that warning in his stomach, he wondered if Abe had found anything else to point to where they were.

He stepped into Frank's office and waited for him to finish his call. Will sat in the chair across from Frank's desk waiting.

"Hey, what's going on?" Shadow asked sitting in the chair next to him.

"Frank is putting the wheels in motion so if Durango wants ransom, he can make a call and the bank will have it within twenty-four hours." Will explained.

"Has he heard anything?" Shadow asked, noting the bags under his friend's eyes.

"So far, no. We only just arrived when the bank returned his call." Will shook his head.

"I'm going to talk with Abe." Shadow said and left the room.

Hawk sat at one of Abe's terminals watching the video of the SUV driving into the car dealership. With the license tag number, they found it. The manager gave them the tapes and the description of the truck Marty bought. Armed with that and the new license plate number, Hawk returned to CFS and Abe let him look through the video until he found the right spot. He watched Marty shake the man's hand and leave in the new dual cab truck.

"Did you find anything?" Shadow asked peering over his shoulder.

"I found the new truck he's driving. I've faxed everything to Josh and he's looking into it." Hawk said.

"Are the girls in the truck with him?" He asked with little hope they were.

"Not that I could tell. Knowing Marty like I do, He's stashed them somewhere. The mere fact that he traded the SUV in Sheridan tells me he's definitely in the area." Hawk said. "We just have to find him."

Shadow let the sliver of hope slip into his heart, but he remained skeptical because of all the terrible things his boss and friends told him about this Durango character. They had to find her and Samantha before the man killed them. Somehow deep down, he surmised the man would keep them alive until he had the money. What he would do after that was anyone's guess.

"Let's head back to Wolf Creek. I need to sleep." Hawk stretched when he stood to his feet.

"We need to stop by Franks office to let him know we're heading back. I'm happy he's allowing us to work on this case instead of the ones he sent the guys out on. I'd go crazy wondering how they progressed on everything." Shadow admitted.

"Man, you got it bad for Elysa, don't you?" Hawk said with a raised brow.

"I didn't expect to be, but she's something special. Don't get me wrong, I'll always love Scarlet Bird, but the Great Spirit has given me a second chance at love." Shadow confessed.

"Some people have all the luck." Hawk shrugged ready to leave. "For the record, I may be jealous, but I'm happy for you."

Frank and Will followed them back to Wolf Creek wondering if Durango had sent them another letter. The waiting proved to be torture for all of them. They also knew Marty's goal to make them suffer wouldn't end anytime soon.

Shadow dropped Hawk off at the house for a nap before the man left for the bar and his usual shift, then drove to his sister's house. He still couldn't believe Josh rented his big house to him so he could be close to Star. He'd missed so much in the years after he left the reservation.

Guilt speared his heart for leaving her behind to deal with Falcon and the other eligible men in the village. There was no excuse for what he did other than he wasn't in a good place when he left. Losing his wife, child, and mother within months of each other did a number on his psyche.

He parked next to the house and walked the long drive to his sister's home. The fresh air revived him, and the peace of the ranch eased the tightness in his chest, although the situation kept him tense.

He slipped inside the door hoping to scare Star, but as always, she knew he was there.

Just before he put his hand on her shoulder, she whirled around, and he wound up looking at the ceiling while Trace barked out a deep belly laugh so loud the baby started crying.

"When are you going to learn my brother, you'll never get the best of me?" She let him up.

"I'll figure out how you know I'm behind you one of these days." He stood up and shook his head.

"I'm gonna start recording you two. I'd make some good money selling copies of the video." Trace wheezed as he rocked his son."

"Tell me you've got some clue as to where Elysa and Samantha are?" Star asked with hope shining in her dark chocolate eyes.

"All we know is he might be in the area. Abe caught a break and found where he'd traded his SUV in for a

truck in Sheridan. That was the last sighting of him."
Shadow explained.

"I'll continue to pray they are found and returned
home safely." Star said swallowing the lump in her
throat. She considered Samantha and Elysa family and
knew how devastated everyone would be if the
unthinkable happened.

"I'll find her and the man that is holding them
captive will pay for every bump and bruise on them."
Shadow declared vehemently.

After dinner, he strolled leisurely to the main house
to rest. When he jumped at the chance to rent it from
the Wolf Brothers, the prospect of marrying Elysa and
having a family with her wasn't far behind the decision.

Before he slid between the cool sheets on his bed,
Shadow knelt to pray like Elysa had done in church.

"Dear Great Spirit

This is Ohanzee and I am new to this kind of prayer,
but Elysa says you listen when she does it. I ask you to
help us find her and Samantha. Stop the madman
holding them from hurting them further.

In Jesus name, Amen."

His eyes closed after climbing into the soft bed.
Somehow, he knew deep down that everything would
be alright.

Chapter Twenty-one

Several days passed after the last contact from
Durango had arrived. Joe finally regained
consciousness but found the swelling of his brain from
the kick in the head blinded him. His life just took the
decision to retire from his hands, it didn't matter that he
wasn't ready for that step.

Josh assumed Joe's position and promoted James to
detective. Now he needed to hire two extra deputies
according to the city council. Even though he and
James were heavily investigating the shooting of the
town and Joe, Josh managed to keep on top of the
normal business dealings.

Shadow sat down with Frank and gave him his
resignation. Josh needed deputies and he was tired of
leaving town every time he turned around. Frank talked
him into staying on until they found Elysa. He knew
Shadow wanted to marry his sister and he approved
wholeheartedly.

Frank sat back in his chair at the home office and
closed his eyes. The strain of the unknown bore down
on him like a thousand-pound weight. Elysa was the
only family he had left other than his wife and children.

Ginger brought the mail in and set it in front of him,
then went to check on the little ones. Since they started
walking, she had her hands full. Thank God Frank
erected a small kiddie corral complete with a swing set
with a slide and a huge sand pile for them to dig in. She
put a huge umbrella over the sand pile so they wouldn't
develop a sunburn from the sweltering summer sun.

Frank's eyes fell on the mail when he opened his
eyes. Ginger learned how to be as quiet as Shadow at
times. When he picked up the stack of letters and bills,
he knew the letter he and Wolf were waiting for rested
somewhere in the stack.

The minute he read it, Will knocked on the door. He hurried to open it to an angry husband who clearly loved Samantha. He'd lost weight and had dark circles under his eyes. With Hoss out healing from his injuries, Will had even more on his plate. Thankfully, Samantha's mother moved in with them after her father passed away. She ran the house and herded the children so Will could function in his daily duties. At times like this he wished he hadn't taken on the mayoral duties of Wolf Creek.

"You got one too?" Frank nodded at envelope in his hand.

"Yup, you?" He growled.

"At least this time we have a date to receive instructions where to deliver the money. How much is he asking from you?" Frank sighed.

"Half a million." He sat down across from Frank in his office.

"That brings the total to two million. I need to go into Sheridan and set the plans in motion." Frank grabbed his keys. "Let me tell Ginger we're leaving."

Will waited at Frank's truck for him. He called Delia and told her what was going on. "I promise mom, I'll get her back safely."

"I trust you Will. Be careful son." His mother-in-law sniffed.

"I will." He replied hoping he could keep that promise.

***

Elysa jumped when Samantha touched her shoulder.

"It's alright, it's just me." She whispered.

"Where are we?" Elysa asked, confused by the new surroundings.

"I don't know, but I'm sure we'll find out soon." She said.

"Speak of the devil." Elysa slid a little closer to Samantha as the lock on the door slid back and the light from above filled the room.

"You'll be happy to know this will all be over by Sunday." Paul told them, enjoying the relief in their faces. "Unfortunately, it will be the last day you'll see your families."

"What do you mean?" The women asked in unison as fear ripped through their hearts.

"You'll find out soon enough." Paul smirked as he set the lunchbox on the ground and left the cellar.

"What do you think he means?" Elysa asked Samantha.

"Either we die, or Frank and Will do." She said honestly. There wasn't any sense in sugarcoating the facts. From everything Will had told her about this man, he was unstable to begin with. After all the years since their testimony put him in prison the anger the man held had festered and he became a monster.

"I never got to tell Shadow how I feel about him." Elysa said with big tears rolling down her smudged dirty cheeks.

"If there's one thing I've learned about Shadow, the man doesn't miss much. I'm quite sure he knows how you feel." Samantha soothed her.

"Wish I had listened to him and Frankie when they tried to tell me the job was dangerous. I had no idea this man was the Marty Frank and Wolfie told us about." Elysa sniffed.

"It's all water under the bridge now. We need to focus and look for an opportunity to escape." Samantha stiffened her back. "God always makes a way of escape. He'll protect us."

"I just wish He'd hurry. I don't know how much more we can take from Marty or Paul." Elysa lamented.

"I'm not so sure they aren't the same person. They're never here at the same time."

"I've been wondering that myself. Will never mentioned he had a twin brother." Samantha agreed. "That could just mean Marty never said anything about him having a twin."

"We'll have to wait to see what he has planned. Either way, if you see an opportunity to get away, do it. Don't worry about me." Samantha ordered. "Promise me."

"I can't leave you behind. They'll kill you." Elysa protested.

"I guess you're right, I couldn't leave you behind either." Samantha sighed. "We'll think of something."

They fell silent as they ate the dry sandwiches their captor provided. At least they weren't starving them unless they were punishing them for some perceived transgression. No matter how this ended, they both kept silent about how they longed for their freedom.

Chapter Twenty-two

Everyone gathered at Frank's house to wait for Marty's call. Abe had set up a remote link to his phone so he could track the signal. At best they would find out where the man had the women, at worst, they'd have to follow his direction to get the money to him.

Shadow, Kevin, and Hawk explained what they wanted to do when they discovered the man's plans.

"We've grown up together in the remotest part of the reservation. That alone taught us to think and react as one." Shadow explained. "When we have a location, let the three of us go in first. You know how quickly and quietly we move. Before Marty even knows were close, we'll have him."

"Let's wait and see how he wants to do this before I decide." Frank said.

The phone's high-pitched ring split the air. Before Frank picked it up, Abe had the number ready to track.

"Hello?"

"Did you get the money?" Marty's gravelly voice asked.

"Yes, where do you want to meet us?" Frank asked.

"I'll text you the directions. You have five hours to meet me with the money. You and Wolf come alone and leave all your guns and ammo behind. If I see anyone else, your women will die." Marty snarled. "Don't jerk me around or they'll wish they'd never been born."

"We'll follow your instructions to the letter. Just don't hurt them." Frank agreed desperately trying to keep the anger out of his voice.

"See you in four hours. Don't be late." Marty ended the call.

"Abe?" Frank looked at the monitor where Abe worked feverishly to pinpoint the call's origins.

Abe told them the coordinates before ending the call.

Will looked over the map of the county and swore. "They're at the Anderson ranch! That madman has kept them under our noses the entire time!"

"Frank, let us do this." Shadow insisted.

"How long will it take you to get ready to go?" Frank looked at Shadow.

"We're ready now." Shadow replied.

"We'll follow you in my truck until we get within a mile of the meeting place. Then we'll travel on foot from there."

"Don't blow your cover. Marty won't hesitate to kill one or both of them." Will spoke up.

"We know what we're doing." Hawk assured his longtime friend.

Silently, they moved from the house to their vehicles. Ginger waved as they left, then she knelt in front of her couch and prayed.

"Dear Lord,

Please watch over them and keep them safe as they find our friends. Give them wisdom and peace while dealing with this crazed maniac.

Amen."

***

Elysa and Samantha watched Marty closely as he brought their lunch to them. After their conversation they paid closer attention to the mannerisms of the two men. So far, the only difference in the two men was when Marty asked if they were okay, he seemed sincere. Paul on the other hand didn't ask about their welfare. He only came to inflict torment upon them or take pictures now and again.

Samantha secretly feared he might sell them off to someone. She regretted watching that special about human trafficking. So, Elysa wouldn't worry, she kept that to herself while praying inside that wouldn't happen.

Finally, Marty left them in total darkness again. There was something different about Marty today. An undercurrent of excitement came through his mannerism. Samantha knew the time Paul often tormented them with grew near. She only hoped they made it out of this alive.

"Samantha, do you think this is almost over? Didn't he seem a little, I don't know, giddy?" Elysa asked.

"Yes, I do. At least I hope so." She answered, keeping the dread she felt out of her voice. Elysa was young and had her entire life ahead of her. Although Samantha didn't want to die, she'd sacrifice herself to keep the young woman alive. She prayed God would help Will forgive her if what she suspected happened.

Left in the darkness, they settled onto the mats to contemplate their situation and how they could stop what they could feel coming on the horizon.

Chapter Twenty-three

Shadow, Hawk and Kevin slipped into the forest between the road and the ranch. Without a sound, the men followed the plan they had formed to the letter.

Soon they could see each other from the dense tree line around the property. The deadline to meet Frank slowly crept up on them as they watched for any sign of movement. They had to know how many men Marty had with him.

***

Elysa tied Samantha up before Marty bound her hands behind her back and forced her up the stairs into the kitchen. After locking the door behind them, he shoved her toward the back door and outside.

"Where are you taking me?" She asked, forgetting the rule about asking questions.

The blow she received knocked her to the ground. Then he jerked her to her feet so hard her arm felt like it was out of socket. Remaining silent though she wanted to scream from the pain, she followed along as he led her to the barn.

After he tied her to the cross tie for the horses, he went back for Samantha.

"Don't try to get away. I'll be back with your friend." Paul growled.

Soon he returned with Samantha and bound her back-to-back with Elysa on the cross tie.

"Relax ladies, this will all be over soon." Paul smirked.

After his retaliation, the women remained silent as he sat on a bale of hay to check his rifles unaware help was just outside the door.

Their question about Marty and Paul didn't appear until Marty surfaced to keep his 'brother' from breaking his word.

"I'm sorry Paul hit you again. You have to stop questioning his actions. I can only do so much to keep him under control, but I fear I'm fighting a losing battle. Each time he surfaces now I find I'm losing myself to him." Marty checked to make sure their bonds weren't too tight. "I never wanted to kidnap you, but Paul had other plans while I slept."

"So, Paul is a part of you?" Samantha asked.

"I guess you could say that. We've always been together since before we were born. When I was little, he had no control over me. My parents thought he was my imaginary friend before they left me on the steps of the police station." Marty opened up. "Wolf and Bear had no idea that Paul was the killing machine on our missions. I don't have the stomach for most of that stuff he did. My mistake was allowing him to join the Military and undergo their harsh training for Special Forces. Now I fear no one will remember who I really am if he takes over."

"If you let us go, we can stop this madness." Samantha insisted as she noticed Shadow slip into the barn with Hawk and Kevin close behind.

"I need the money Frank is bringing to me. With that, I'll disappear for good." Marty grabbed his throbbing head. Paul was really making it difficult for him to stay in control.

Paul surfaced without warning and put the rifle to Elysa's head. "One more step and she's dead!"

"Release them, you can't get all of us." Hawk growled.

"Well, well, well. If it ain't my old buddy Hawk. I should have known you'd follow Bear and Wolf wherever they went." Paul chuckled, lowering the rifle to turn it on Hawk.

"Come on Marty, let the women go. Hurting them won't stop the day of reckoning coming for you." Hawk tried to reason with him. "Wolf and Bear will be here with your money soon and we can all return to our lives again."

"You never understood that Marty is a weak sniveling idiot. If it weren't for me, he'd have died that first mission we were on together." Paul insisted.

"Um, what are you saying?" Hawk's eyebrows shot up under his hairline.

"I'm not Marty. I'm Paul his brother." The man smirked.

While Hawk kept him busy, Shadow slipped behind the girls and cut their bonds. The second they moved to get away Hawk lunged at Marty and the rifle fired knocking Hawk to the ground. Shadow's knife sunk into Marty's chest as he whirled around to shoot Elysa.

A moment later, Frank and Will burst into the barn upon hearing the rifle shot as Shadow knelt beside Hawk. He and Frank tried to stop the bleeding, but the bullet hit an artery.

"Don't you die on me Hawk!" Shadow shouted. "Keep your eyes on me!"

"Tell Star I love her." Hawk wheezed.

"Why didn't you let us disarm him before attacking him?" Shadow asked as the lump in his throat grew painful.

"You have a life to make with Elysa. I don't have anyone to love me like that. I've always been too late to get the girl." Hawk's voice grew faint as his eyes glazed over.

"Fight Hawk!" Shadow bellowed still applying pressure to the man's wound.

"It's too late, he's gone." Frank and Kevin put a hand on his shoulders.

Sirens wailed in the distance as Frank and Will wrapped the women into their arms and comforted them while the paramedics arrived to checked on everyone's injures.

In the end they transported Samantha and Elysa to the hospital. Frank and Will followed them while Shadow and Kevin waited with Josh until the coroner's hearse arrived.

While waiting the blood brothers stood over Hawk's lifeless body and cut a huge lock of hair from their heads then ran the blade of their knives across their chest in the Lakota signs of grief.

Doc followed the young orderly who helped in the morgue into the barn and hurried to help the two men.

"It's okay Doc." Shadow moved away from his probing fingers. "It's our tradition, we'll be fine."

After they helped load Hawk and Marty into the hearse, they walked back to Shadow's truck in silence. The events of this day will live on in their hearts forever.

Chapter Twenty-four

Elysa sat up in the hospital bed wishing the doctor would let her go home. She knew that Samantha was in another room down the hall.

It didn't matter that she felt fine, especially after the long hot shower she indulged in. To say it felt phenomenal to stand under the hot spray was an understatement. Now that she was clean and full from the hamburger and fries the nurse brought her for dinner, she wanted to just go home and sit outside for a long while.

Explaining the feeling of being out in the sunshine after two months of living in a dungeon was difficult. At least she knew someone who understood since Samantha experienced it with her.

The sharp knock on the door shook her from the memories haunting her. "Come in."

Frank rushed in with Ginger and four toddlers. The smiles on their faces when they saw her brought tears to her eyes. How close had she come to being unable to cuddle the little ones ever again? When her brother's eyes met hers, she knew he understood her mindset.

Ginger hugged her so tightly she couldn't breathe, but it felt so good she wouldn't stop her. Her sister-in-law meant the world to her. She finally had the sister she'd always wanted.

Frank pulled Ginger away and gathered her in his arms. In that moment, all the fear, pain, and misery she suffered broke loose from the dam she held them behind. Frank soothed her while Ginger occupied the little ones who started crying along with her.

Finally, exhausted from releasing her emotions, she mopped her face with the last tissue in the box the nurse had opened after they put her in the room.

"Where is Samantha?" She managed to ask.

"In the next room. She's okay too." Frank said.

"How are Shadow and Kevin?" She sniffed still in shock that Hawk had given his life for her and Samantha.

"They're grieving. I think Shadow is taking it harder than Kevin is. We'll all miss him." Frank responded sadly.

"I can't believe Hawk took the bullet to save me and Samantha." She shook her head.

"I'm taking the kids home, and Ginger will stay with you." Frank insisted.

"You don't need to do that. I'll be okay. Besides, you wouldn't get any rest with them waking us up a hundred times at night for vitals and stuff." She shook her head.

"If, you're sure." Ginger said.

"Positive, I'm sure there will be several visitors before they close the doors at nine." She tried to sound upbeat.

"I'll come by in the morning." Frank hugged her again after Ginger squeezed the air out of her lungs again.

After they left Elysa thought how gracious God was to her and Ginger. They both desired a sister their entire lives and now they have each other. Samantha quickly earned that status too, at least for her. She and Ginger were already sisters at heart and after what Marty had put them through a special bond formed between them.

Josh stopped in a few minutes after Frank left to take her statement and visit for a few minutes. When he saw her, she started crying again. They were good friends, and she knew she could trust him.

He sat down on the side of her bed and held her while she cried.

"Sh. It's all over now. Marty is dead and won't bother anyone again." He soothed her.

"You'd think I wouldn't have any tears left after breaking down with Frank." She cleared the tears with a washcloth.

When she sat back against the pillows, he began questioning her about the ordeal she escaped from.

"I didn't know who Marty really was until after he kidnapped me. When I woke up from the chloroform, he dosed me with, I realized the mistake I'd made." She went on to tell him the same story Samantha told him. "We had no idea the man had a split personality until he tied up in the barn. Samantha noticed the subtle differences in their demeanor each time he brought us food or took our pictures." She finished her statement.

Josh stood to leave after a short conversation about her stubborn idea she was invincible.

***

Shadow stood out of sight in the hallway at Elysa's door. In his frame of mind, he forgot Josh had married Jillian and left without a sound.

Jumping into his truck he drove to his sister's house. No one understood him like she did.

Rolling to a stop in the drive, he ran past the barn and onto her porch. She opened the door before he could knock.

"I…" He couldn't say anymore. He would never cry in front of her, but losing Hawk and now Elysa, he couldn't bear the weight of the emotional turmoil ripping his insides apart.

"*Ohanzee*? What's wrong?" She wrapped her arms around him.

"Hawk's dead and Elysa found someone else." He managed.

"What happened to Hawk? And who did Elysa find?" She asked as tears gathered in her eyes.

He sat down at the kitchen table next to her and explained everything. "Hawk wanted you to know he loved you."

"I knew he loved me, but our paths were meant to go in different directions. In a way I loved him too." Star admitted. "But not the way I love Trace."

"Why do you think I didn't let him date you?" Shadow smirked sadly. "I'll miss him."

"Now tell me about Elysa?" Star insisted.

"I saw them together at the hospital." Shadow told her. "It's plain to see they have something special."

"I know she loves you, my brother. You forget not only is Josh married, but they are close friends." Star reminded him. "I'm sure you're misreading the entire situation."

"No matter, I have to go back to the reservation and let Hawk's family know he's dead. I won't be back for few days." He stood to leave.

"Won't Frank be upset you are gone?" Star asked worried he would lose his job.

"No, I've given him my resignation. When I return, I'll talk to Josh about working as a deputy. I'm weary of the out of state cases. I want to settle down here and..." He stopped speaking.

"You had plans to ask her to marry you, didn't you?" Star understood his devastation now.

"I'll figure it out later. For now, I need to be on my way." Shadow said as Star hugged him again. "I'll be back in a few days if anyone wants to know."

Star watched her brother get into his truck and said a prayer that his heart would heal while he was away. The death of Hawk was one thing but the brief thought of losing Elysa to another man caused such severe damage that he may never recover from, especially after losing Red Bird and their child. Deep down she knew when he returned things would get interesting.

Chapter Twenty-five

Elysa basked in the bright sunlight as she lounged on the deck at her brother's home. One thing she learned through her and Samantha's ordeal, never, ever take things for granted. It could all go away in the blink of an eye.

Her eyes focused on Ginger playing with her children in the enclosed playground, Frank insisted they needed to corral the toddlers. Elysa could see it had its merits, especially when the four toddlers ran in different directions at the same time.

A smile graced her face when Amelia threw a shovel full of sand into the air. Ginger was going to have a wonderful time getting that out of her hair.

Her attention turned toward the driveway where Trace parked his truck behind Ginger's SUV. Her heart raced hoping Shadow tagged along since he quit working for Frank.

When Star took little Allen from his seat in the back, Trace shut the door and kissed her before leaving to finish working the ranch with Will.

"Hi Star!" Ginger called out. "Bring Allen on over."

Star put the little one down in the sandpile as Elysa watched the babies play. Her heart ached to have what her friend and sister-in-law had. She felt even more disheartened, wishing Shadow would be the one to share the rest of her life with.

Star's shadow fell across her drawing her attention from her daydreaming.

"Hi, how are you feeling." Star said sitting next to her while Ginger watched Allen for a few minutes.

"I'm good. The sunshine feels heavenly." She replied.

"Samantha said the same thing when I saw her earlier." Star grinned.

"How's Shadow handling losing Hawk?" She asked sadly.

"Not well. He went to the reservation to tell Hawk's family." Star watched her closely.

"Oh. Did he say when he would be back?" She tried to sound normal even though her pulse rate increased.

"He didn't know." Star debated what to say. "So, you and Josh are an item now?"

"What? NO! Whoever told you that is dead wrong, besides, he's happily married to Jillian. I would never step into someone else's relationship like that." She sat up in shock. "How could you think that of me?"

"Shadow saw you in Josh's arms at the hospital when he stopped in last night. He assumed..." Star shrugged.

"That silly man. I've already explained my relationship with Josh to him." She fell back against the deck chair. "So, he left believing I was with Josh then?"

"I reminded him Josh was married. I think in his frame of mind he couldn't see anything too clearly. He and Hawk were inseparable as young braves. Those two created more havoc for our mothers than any other children in the village." Star smiled sadly. "After Falcon murdered Scarlet Bird, Shadow's wife, and son, then losing our mother, he left without a word to anyone. Hawk left after Scarlet Bird and Shadow married so we figured he went looking for him. Until I left the reservation no one knew where he was."

"I'm sorry for the loss of your mother." She reached out and grasped Star's hand.

"Thank you, she's with the Great Spirit now so I'm happy for her." Star said. "I better go help Ginger with the little ones. Why don't you join us?"

"I think I will." She replied standing to follow. Later when she had time alone, she would mull over what Star had revealed about Shadow.

The afternoon brought with it a peaceful silence in the house. The babies slept soundly after lunch giving the three women time to relax before they awakened for dinner.

Later that evening, Elysa soaked in a hot tub to go over the conversation with Star. One thing for certain she needed to speak with Josh before Shadow came back. Deep down she feared he may never return if Star was right.

Weary from the day, she slipped between the sheets hoping to sleep better than she had since her kidnapping. With a yawn and a prayer, she went to sleep dreaming about Shadow.

Chapter Twenty-six

Shadow parked his truck in front of Hawk's family home. It wasn't much to look at, but Hawk's family made it work. *Chapawee*, (Industrious), Hawk's mother sat in a worn rocker on the small porch of the home.

"*Ohanzee*?" She looked up in surprise. "Why are you here?"

"Is *Wapasha*, (Red Leaf), here?" He asked her son, *Enapay*, (Appears Bravely).

"He is hunting." *Chapawee* answered warily. "Have you seen my son?"

"That is why I'm here. *Chayton*, (Hawk), sleeps with the Great Spirit." Shadow answered.

Chapawee wailed as she drew her knife and cut her long braid from her head. Her son followed and cut his bare chest after taking a sizable chunk of his long black hair.

Shadow waited with them in silence until *Wapasha* returned. After a short conversation, Shadow refused the offer of dinner and left for his childhood home at the other end of the community.

After he cut the engine of his truck, he sat looking at the home he grew up in. Unable to hold back the memories of his childhood with Hawk broke free as tears slid down his cheeks. Alone in the truck, he allowed that grief to blanket him. There were no regrets for keeping him from dating his sister, yet his heart hurt that Hawk couldn't find his heartmate.

He knew Hawk had also loved Scarlet Bird. Hawk wouldn't have said anything to him. Now his blood brother was gone. The conversation with his parents about his remains meant he would have to return sooner than he wanted. He needed time to heal from his losses.

No matter what Star said, Josh was a bit too familiar with Elysa. If you are married, you should never touch another woman like that. Deep down he knew he was only protecting himself from further heartache. Better to start now than wait until he gave his heart to her and have her refuse it.

Weary of the direction his mind took, he grabbed his small backpack, lantern, and sleeping bag before he went inside. Unprepared for the destruction inside, he stood in the doorway with the small lantern in shock.

The place looked ransacked. Even the back door and the door to Star's room were missing as well as some windows. He understood the need for those items on the reservation and couldn't fault whoever took them.

With a heavy sigh, he moved a few things around and made a nest of sorts with his sleeping bag. Although he tried to sleep, it eluded him again. Every time he closed his eyes, memories would flood his mind.

Close to dawn, he gathered his things and put them in his truck. Before leaving he had to visit the graves of his wife, son, and parents. He was thankful that Kevin had overseen the burial of his father. The man knew it would've taken time to find him and Star, so he made all the arrangements before setting out to find them.

Shadow passed by the stream that ran through his father's land setting his memory free again. This place held so many adventures for him, Hawk and Kevin. Even though Kevin was a bit older, he still joined in some of their more exciting excursions. Star would tag along at times as well, but her friendship with Scarlet Bird took precedence over their fun.

The overgrown cemetery came into view as he stopped at the top of the small hill. His heart ached as he made his way down past the older tombstones to the newer ones. It didn't take long to locate his family's graves.

He sat at the foot of them and wept bitter tears over the many losses he endured. After his tears dried, a cool breeze lifted his hair as the grass bowed to its strength.

Shadow raised his eyes to the horizon and saw his parents, his wife and son, and Hawk standing before him.

"Please don't grieve any longer for us. We are happy and waiting for the day when you join us and the Great Spirit." Scarlet Bird whispered.

"How can I not? Only my sister keeps me here. If not for her…" Shadow shook his head.

"You have another. Elysa loves you my blood brother, don't let her slip away or my death will mean nothing." Hawk said. "I'm here taking care of your family until your time comes to an end."

"We love you." His parents waved as the apparitions faded away.

Shadow sat for a long while before he returned to the shack. He stopped at the council hall on his way back to Wolf Creek. He gave them the authority to use whatever they needed from the property.

Much to the council elder's disappointment, Shadow turned down the job Kevin had vacated a few years ago. He considered it carefully, but he knew it wasn't his desire any more now than when he left the first time.

When he drove past Widow's Bend, he called Josh and asked to see him when he arrived back in town. After he talked with him about Elysa. The answers Josh gave him would determine if he applied for the position of deputy.

If he had his sights on Elysa, he wouldn't work for him. If the man cheated on his wife, he couldn't trust him. His heart hurt thinking Elysa was in love with Josh and vice versa. Maybe his sister was right, maybe he misread the situation. The only answer to that lay with Josh and he would settle that first thing.

Almost an hour later, Shadow parked in front of the new police station. As he got out of his truck, he squared his shoulders ready to do battle if necessary.

Chapter Twenty-seven

Josh sat in his office with a shocked expression frozen on his face. The angry Lakota glared at him waiting for an answer.

"Well? Are you leaving your wife for Elysa?" Shadow repeated the question.

"What makes you think I'm leaving my pregnant wife for Elysa?" Josh finally responded.

"I saw you comforting her the night we found her." Shadow replied angrily. "If you want her, I'll have to fight you for her."

"Look, I don't know what you think you saw, but I have no designs on Elysa. We dated for a few months and realized we weren't meant to be together. The only feelings I have for her are pure friendship." Josh retorted. "There is no need to fight me for her hand."

"I believe you." Shadow relaxed. "If you won't hold this against me, I'd like to apply for one of the deputy positions you have open."

"I have no problem at all with that. You're hired, all you have to do is fill out the paperwork, then we'll get you a uniform and the standard equipment for the job. You'll have to use your personal truck, but we'll give you a stipend for the wear and tear along with gas privileges." Josh said, then gave him the rate of pay.

"I accept. When do you want me to start?" Shadow agreed.

"A week from Monday at seven a.m. We'll start with desk duty for a few days to get you used to our paperwork and how we do things around here." Josh replied. "What did you find out about Hawk's remains?"

"His family gave permission to have him cremated so they can take him home. They are poor people without the means to bring him back home in a coffin."

Shadow said. "I'll stop at the funeral home when I leave here. After the arrangements, I'll make another trip to the reservation and bring his immediate family back with me. They can stay at the ranch since I'm the only one living there."

"Keep us posted for the proceedings." Josh said, handing him the paperwork and leading him to the interrogation room to fill it out.

"Okay." Shadow followed hoping it wouldn't take too long.

Soon Shadow stood in the small funeral parlor. Three coffins sat on display. He promised Hawks family he would take care of everything.

"As you can see these are top of the line, with silk lining. This one has brass handles, and the mahogany stained wood has three coats of polyurethane for the highly polished look." The mortician gave him the sales pitch.

"Although these are beautiful, the family wishes to cremate him." He pointed to the bronze-colored metal urn.

"Excellent choice." The man smiled from ear to ear and explained the price included, the funeral announcement too. "We can also put him in a rental casket for the funeral and cremate him afterward."

"I like that idea, how much for everything?" Shadow pulled out his wallet.

After he paid the man, he went to the small church at the edge of town.

Pastor Jones greeted him from the small bed of flowers in front of the church. "How can I help you?"

"I'm in need of your services for a funeral." Shadow explained.

The two men talked through the ceremony and if he had a preference of who read the eulogy. He gave him the information for the florist in town to deliver the flowers he needed.

His next stop was the safehouse to gather Hawks personal items. Like the rest of the single employees of CFS, Hawk had very few possessions.

With everything Hawk owned in two backpacks, he went back to the funeral home to give the items to the mortician to dress him in. In keeping with their Lakota heritage, he picked out the traditional leggings and shirt of the Lakota warriors.

From there he made the floral arrangements and stopped to give Josh the date and time of the funeral.

Once again, his truck traveled back to the reservation to help Hawk's family buy clothes for the funeral and to bring them back to Wolf Creek with him.

While packing his things, he found a small leather pouch that had a sizeable life insurance policy with his parents named as sole beneficiary. Nevertheless, Shadow would pay for everything. He owed more than his life to Hawk. The man sacrifice himself for Shadow's happiness and he would never be able to repay what his blood brother had done for him.

Chapter Twenty-eight

Elysa's heart fell while listening to Frank tell Ginger about Hawk's impending funeral. When he explained Shadow went back to the reservation to bring Hawk's family back with him, her heart ached with longing to see him.

There was so much she wanted to tell him, but since they had rescued her and Samantha, Shadow was so busy he hadn't called or stopped in to see her. Before Marty had kidnapped her; she suspected Shadow wanted to date her. Now she wondered if she had imagined everything.

"Sis?" Frank waved his hand in front of her face startling her.

"Huh? Sorry, what did you say?" She shook her head as her face heated.

"I want to know if you're going to accept Josh's offer of photographer?" Frank asked again.

"I think so. I think it would be an interesting job." She answered.

"Have you ever thought about being a forensic scientist?" Ginger asked.

"Not really. I'll see how I do with taking pictures first. If it interests me, I'll look into it." She said.

"Don't wait too long to talk to him, he'll advertise out of town if you don't accept." Frank warned her.

"Okay." She sighed. "When will Shadow be back?"

"I don't know." Frank shrugged. "He quit after Hawk died."

"He what?" Elysa sat straighter in shock. "He loves his job."

"After Hawk died, he came in and quit. Something in him broke when Hawk passed." Frank said.

"So, he may never come back?" Her heart cracked a little more.

"You didn't hear me say he's bringing Hawk's family back for the funeral?" Frank grinned.

"Shut up!" She swatted his arm.

"Just so you know, I approve." Frank smiled affectionately. "With him around I won't worry so much about you."

"Obviously, you were right to worry about me. I shoulda listened to you and Shadow." Elysa snorted. "Maybe working with Josh will be a safer job."

"You won't have to worry about anything but taking pictures of dead people." Frank grinned when she showed how repulsive that thought was.

"I guess I'll talk to Josh about the job. Can I borrow your truck?" Elysa asked.

"I'm going to the safe house to work; I'll drop you off." Frank kissed Ginger's cheek.

"I need to find something to get around in. I don't wanna borrow your car all the time." Elysa followed him outside. "I may even need to find a place to live soon. I can't sponge off of you and Ginger all the time."

"Shadow might take care of the living situation soon, as far as a car, I'll take you this weekend to look for one." Frank helped her into his truck.

"Okay." She sat back and let her mind wander to Shadow. Where was he and what was he doing?

***

Shadow helped Hawk's mother, *Chapawee*, brother, *Enapay* and older sister, *Kimimela* (Butterfly) into the back of the SUV he rented to transport his family to and from the reservation. Hawk's father, *Wapasha*, sat up front with him for the journey to Wolf Creek.

During their journey, *Wapasha*, grilled him on how his son had died.

"He died with honor while saving a life." Shadow said simply.

When they arrived at Wolf Creek, he stopped at the small diner to feed his dear friends. Growing up with them was an honor and he thought of the siblings as family to him. During his teenage years he had such a crush on *Kimimela*, he often angered her with his childish pranks.

The minute he met Scarlet Bird, *Kimimela* took second place in his heart. He knew it was a relief to *Kimimela* when he turned his attention to the woman he eventually married.

After taking their seats, the waitress took their order as the family looked around the area. Several of the regulars kept sneaking curious glances toward them.

Their meals arrived and they dug into the delicious food with gusto. He knew they only ate what they could hunt or grow on the reservation. Now that Hawk had left everything to his family, he suspicioned they would think of moving to a more developed area on the reservation.

When they finished their meal, Shadow escorted them to the ranch where they would stay until after the funeral. He showed them to the rooms they would sleep in and called Star to let her know they had arrived.

Star insisted he bring them to her house for the dinner she currently slaved over in anticipation of seeing her long-time friend *Kimimela*.

Shadow took *Kimimela* and *Enapay* to the barn to show them the horses Trace was currently training. They watched in fascination as Trace put the young colts through their paces.

The look on his friend's faces when Trace greeted them in Lakota then asked various questions in their language sent him into a fit of laughter.

Chapter Twenty-nine

Elysa sat across from Josh in his office listening to him explain what her job would entail after offering her the position.

"The most important thing about your job is making sure every picture is clear and recorded at the crime scene. I know you don't have the scientific background to fully investigate, but we'll worry about that later." Josh explained.

"Just how bad are the crime scenes?" She asked curiously.

"Most aren't too bad, however, there have been a few truly gruesome ones since I started as a deputy. Then there are the ones that have decomposing bodies. Those are the really bad ones that will turn your stomach." Josh continued. "Can you manage that?"

"I've been helping Ginger change four babies that have some pretty awful diapers. Not to mention the fact that I've seen calves and horses give birth. If it's too bad, I'll learn to deal with it." She replied. "Besides, I need to get my own place before long. Frank is taking me to get a car this weekend."

"May I suggest you get a SUV with four-wheel-drive?" Josh said. "It's big enough to carry any extra supplies you may need and sturdy enough to maneuver some of the rough terrain around here."

"I'll keep that in mind." She said.

"You'll receive health insurance, and an allowance for using your own vehicle." Josh informed her then gave her the starting salary. "You'll get a raise after ninety days."

"Thank you for hiring me Josh." She accepted the file of paperwork to fill out.

"You start next Monday." He stood and shook her hand. "You can fill those out down the hall in the breakroom."

Elysa left to do just that. Thirty minutes later, she walked to the safehouse where Frank collaborated remotely with his entire company.

He looked up when she walked in. "Hey, how did it go?"

"I start Monday." She smiled happily.

"That makes sense, Hawk's funeral is tomorrow. Everyone is closing for the ceremony." Frank's voice cracked.

"I'm sorry you lost your friend. I'll miss him too. He always had everyone in tears with his practical jokes." Elysa blinked back the tears stinging her eyes.

"I'll never forget the joke that backfired on him before Ginger, and I got together. I played it up the entire ride to the airport. Just before they took off for the job, I called and told him I was kidding. Neal and Justice were laughing in the background when he swore." Frank smiled sadly at the memory.

"Are you about finished? I'd like to get back and help Ginger with the kiddos." She changed the subject.

"Let me wrap up everything with Abe. It shouldn't take me long." He began typing on his laptop.

Elysa sat down on the couch to wait. Her conversation with Star about Shadow replayed in her mind. A small snort escaped when she thought about him seeing her in Josh's arms.

"Silly man." She murmured.

"Who's a silly man?" Frank asked, closing his laptop.

"No one." She replied unwilling to get into anything involving Shadow and her brother.

"You ready to go?" He asked, grabbing his briefcase.

"Yup." She went to the door.

Elysa fell silent on the way back to Frank's house. Her mind whirling around how Star thought he had feelings for her. In her own case, she had fallen head over heels for the man. For one moment she allowed her fantasy of having him for a husband and a brood of little Lakota running around.

When Frank parked the car, she went inside to pick out an outfit for Hawks funeral in the morning. She was happy to hear Dillon's wife would watch all the children with Samantha's mother, freeing up those who wanted to attend. She still couldn't believe what Ginger told her about Dillon's first wife. From what she could tell, Dillon was a happily married man now.

Dinner was noisy and fun with the little ones learning to feed themselves. Deep down her heart ached for the happiness her brother had found with Ginger. Oh, they had an explosive courtship, but in the end, they overcame all the drama surrounding them. Now they were happy like her parents had been.

After helping clean up the dining room and kitchen, Elysa went upstairs to take a long hot bath before going to bed.

Frank closed the bedroom door with mixed emotions. He was happy for her, but he had to worry a little bit about Shadow. If the man desired to do so, he could potentially hurt his sister.

"She's pining for Shadow, isn't she?" Ginger asked wrapping her arms around her husband when he crawled into bed.

"It seems that way." Frank kissed her shoulder. "He better not break her heart."

"You know Shadow better than that. Besides, Star wouldn't let him hurt her." Ginger laid her head on his chest.

"I got news for you Red. Star will side with her brother no matter what." He ran his fingers through her hair.

"Star won't let him pull any shenanigans on Elysa." She yawned.

They cuddled up together and fell asleep dreading the funeral on the horizon.

Chapter Thirty

The morning brought an overcast sky mirroring the emotions of the friends and family of Gary Allen Hawk. The tiny church was filled to capacity with standing room only. After everyone took their seats, the family filed in and sat in the reserved seats up front.

Shadow escorted a beautiful young Lakota woman behind Hawk's parents and younger brother. Shadow sat next to her while Trace and Star sat on the other side.

The preacher stood behind the large wooden pulpit and said an opening prayer, then music came on. 'Broken Halo's' by Chris Stapleton played softly as a picture of Hawk was displayed on the screen behind the preacher.

After Frank read the eulogy, the song 'Angels Among Us' by Alabama drifted over the crowd.

The preacher said all the comforting words and reminded them that Hawk was in Heaven and would see us one day. Then while they opened the casket for viewing, the song 'One More Day' by Diamond Rio played softly in the background.

Row by row people streamed to the front to see Hawk one last time. Elysa walked next to Jarod as Frank and Ginger went ahead of them. Jarod steadied her as she stumbled through her tears.

Shadow's jaw clenched as he watched them. First it was Josh, now she's with Jarod? How could he be such a fool. He waited too long to ask her out, now he'd lost her.

After everyone had passed by and left the room for the family to say goodbye, *Kimimela* stood, and he jumped to his feet to escort her past the casket.

Tears fell from the old couple as they wept over their son. Shadow stood strong for the family since he had already grieved for his blood brother. Now, even though he gave up the right to be chief, he stood proudly by the family as his father would have expected him to.

***

Elysa watched as Shadow escorted the lovely Lakota woman out of the chapel while Frank, Will, Neal, Carl, Tank and Justice dressed in their military uniforms carried the casket out to the hearse. They watched it leave as the pastor announced the luncheon for the family at Will Wolf's home.

"You ready sis?" Frank asked.

"I think I'll just go home." She muttered while wiping tears from her eyes.

"You're just gonna let that woman steal him away?" Ginger cut in. "If you want him, you're gonna have to fight for him Elysa."

"Maybe. But today isn't the time or place for that." Elysa shrugged.

"You're going to go with us and hold your head high. If Shadow has any feelings at all for you, he'll come around. But if you go into hiding, he may just leave for good." Ginger insisted.

"Okay." Elysa gave in, wondering how she would make it through the afternoon watching Shadow and the other woman.

***

The somber mood hung heavy in the air at the Wolf Ranch. Like Frank, Hawk had become one of the town citizens. No one had a negative word to say about him.

Elysa stepped from Frank's truck as he opened the door for Ginger. Her heart ached with disappointment and apprehension. She didn't want Shadow to flaunt the Lakota woman in her face. How on earth could she face them knowing in her heart she loved Shadow.

124

Her head told her she should be happy for him, but her heart had other ideas. Ever since she met the Lakota brave, she knew he was the one for her. Even though she didn't want to be here, she squared her shoulders, put on a brave smile, and followed Ginger and Frank inside Will's home.

Samantha and Jillian put Ginger and Elysa to work the minute they arrived. She sent Frank outside with more steaks for her husband to grill while Josh and Trace finished setting up chairs and tables. Star busied herself putting linens on the tables already in place.

Elysa set the silverware and plates on the table by the grill while the other women put the food out. By the time the family arrived along with those closest to Hawk, everything was in place.

Unaware that eyes were on him, Shadow caught *Kimimela* when she stumbled from the SUV.

"Are you okay?" He asked while steadying her on her feet.

"Yes, my foot caught on the matt protecting the carpet." She blushed shyly.

Shadow didn't know, she'd always had a crush on him, but being a bit older she didn't act on it. Besides, Hawk was his best friend, and she wouldn't go there then, but now?

"Take my arm." Shadow insisted as he led everyone to the back yard.

Elysa slipped into the kitchen before they made their appearance. Watching the woman fall into Shadow's arms broke something inside her. Clearly, he had feelings for the beautiful maiden.

She locked herself in the upstairs bathroom for a few minutes to gather her composure, hoping everyone would believe her red eyes were from grieving for Hawk. They didn't need to know exactly why she cried.

Ginger knocked on the door, "Come on out Elysa. Don't you let that woman win Shadow's heart."

"It looked to me like she already has." Elysa sniffed opening the door.

"You know they all grew up together, if she meant anything to him, Shadow wouldn't have married Scarlet Bird." Ginger told her. "Now wash your face and join the rest of us."

Elysa reluctantly obeyed her sister-in-law. With a last look in the mirror, she couldn't help but notice the differences between her and the other woman. While the Lakota maiden's raven black hair, striking brown eyes, and naturally tanned skin enhanced her natural beauty, Elysa had returned to her naturally chocolate brown hair, brown eyes and pale skin were complete opposites.

Chapter Thirty-One

Everyone had just sat down to eat before she joined them. When she looked, she found the only seat open to eat was next to Shadow. Somehow, she had a feeling Ginger arranged for that seat to be empty putting her in an awkward situation.

Shadow jumped up and pulled out her chair as the Lakota woman sized her up.

"Thanks, Shadow." She sat down and placed the napkin in her lap.

"How are you?" He asked, realizing he missed her more than he thought.

"Great, well except for mourning Hawk." She managed.

"We'll all miss him, but he's with the Great Spirit watching over Scarlet Bird and my son." He replied quietly.

Elysa had no idea how to respond to his statement, so she nodded and shoveled a big fork full of potato salad into her mouth.

The conversation going on around her faded into the atmosphere without registering in her mind. When she finished eating, she jumped up and went to get rid of her trash, then migrated toward the sweets. Oh, dear Lord how she needed cake, or pie, or anything else that would comfort her aching heart.

Shadow slipped up behind her while she perused the eight-foot table of decadent desserts.

"What looks good?" Shadow asked startling her into dropping the slice of cake onto the table.

"Don't do that! Look what you made me do!" She whirled around and shook her finger at him.

"Sorry. I didn't mean to startle you." He bit back a grin. One of the many things he loved about her, she was adorable when she got angry.

"Tell it to someone who cares." She murmured cleaning up the mess she'd made. "You should take your friend some of the peach cobbler, I'm sure she'll like it."

"She can get her own pie, or cake. I want to ask you something." He said.

"What would that be?" She eyed him suspiciously.

"I want to take you out on a date when I return from taking Hawk's family home." He gave her the smile that always melted her heart.

"Sorry. I can't." She declined.

"Why not?" His face fell.

"My new job starts Monday and I'll be busy learning the ropes." She declined.

"Oh. Well, some other time then." He replied sullenly before grabbing a plate full of sweets and returning to his seat.

Elysa managed to snag a seat next to Jarod when she returned to the table.

"Hey, how's everything?" She asked with a forced smile.

"Same as always. I've been getting the fields ready to plant oats and corn for feed this winter. Of course, we've got plenty of hay coming up. What about you?"

"I'm starting my new job Monday. Josh hired me to photograph his crime scenes. If I like what I see, he's gonna train me to investigate things." She forgot about Shadow and his friend.

"That sounds impressive. You'll do a fantastic job." Jarod smiled. "How are you since you were kidnapped?"

"I'm okay. It helps since Frank and Ginger know what I'm going through. I think Samantha has been the one who helped me the most. She'd already gone through that once before." Elysa replied honestly.

"I'm glad they found y'all. Frank nearly went bonkers looking for you. Shadow came over nearly every evening hoping someone had contacted him." Jarod said.

"I guess I should get up and help Samantha clean up." She stood and moved away from him.

Jarod caught the look on Shadow's face when he glanced his way. A cold chill inched its way down his spine when he met his eyes. If he didn't know better, he thought Shadow may be a bit jealous, but the deadly look he witnessed gave him pause. Maybe he should keep his distance from Elysa.

Shadow's eyes left Jarod's and followed Elysa as she disappeared into the house.

"She's very pretty." *Kimimela* commented.

"Yes, she is." Shadow tore his eyes away from the door that closed behind her.

"Are y'all ready to go now?" Shadow directed his attention to her parents.

When Hawk's mother nodded, he cleared their place settings and threw everything away. Josh stood near the trash can when he tossed the trash away.

"So, that's Hawk's sister?" He asked.

"Yes. I will take them home in a few days, after I show them around Wolf Creek and Sheridan. We also have to meet with the lawyer handling Hawk's will." Shadow told him. "I'll be back in time to begin working for you."

"I didn't doubt that for a minute." Josh grinned. "I think Jarod has a little crush on Hawk's sister."

"She's older than I am. Jarod needs someone closer to his age. Besides, she'll never leave the reservation as long as her parents are alive." Shadow told him.

"From what I see, she's got a thing for you." Josh observed the woman who kept her eyes on Shadow's every movement.

"Since growing up thinking of her as family, there will never be anything between us." Shadow shook his head.

"Well, you might wanna set her straight, she's been drooling over you all afternoon." Josh clasped his shoulder.

"I hadn't noticed." Shadow replied honestly. "I need to get them home so they can rest. I'll see you a week from Monday. Josh stood by and watched Shadow help the family into the rental SUV. With his keen powers of observation, he could tell the young Lakota woman was smitten with Shadow. He just hoped that Shadow wouldn't hurt Elysa.

Chapter Thirty-two

Monday morning Elysa stepped into the police station ready to go to work. Josh explained her other duties when they were slow. "You'll help Kelly with filing and relieve her for breaks unless a case comes up. Your hours will be eleven to three for now unless we need you to take pictures of a crime scene after hours."

"I can manage that." Elysa replied.

"Today you train with Kelly. She'll get you acquainted with her job." Josh said. "Welcome to the team."

Elysa sat with Kelly as she showed her how to work the radio and manage the phones. When the first lull in the reception area came around, Kelly handed her a box full of folders to file away. She showed her the filing system, then she went back to the front desk.

"We'll take a break at noon; we'll have to eat here since the others are out directing traffic from the last of the funerals from the shooting. They're burying Ethel and Sadie today." Kelly explained.

"Josh used to tell me about those two. He said they were a handful when they got into it over their cat and dog." Elysa smiled sadly. "I think everyone will miss them."

The day turned out to be a busy one with all the people visiting to mourn the loss of loved ones. Some of the stores stayed open to cash in on the out of towners.

The tragedy of so many lives lost the day Marty/Paul Durango fired upon the peaceful small town, will live in their hearts forever.

***

Shadow helped *Kimimela* onto Snowball, one of the three horses Josh left behind when he moved to the ranch he and his new wife now owned.

Enapay stayed with his parents and played the video games Shadow had introduced him to the night before. The kid would miss them when he returned to his home.

Shadow swung onto the back of Cannon Ball, one of Diablo's offspring. Will sold him to Shadow just before Elysa went missing. His heart ached over her rejection. He thought maybe after taking Hawk's family back to the reservation, he would ask her again. If she turned him down again, he would know she had no feelings for him.

"Wanna race?" *Kimimela* asked when they cleared the fenced off sections of the ranch.

"Go!" Shadow kicked Cannon Ball into action. Snowball had no chance of beating him since she was much older than his horse.

When the creek came into view Shadow slowed to allow *Kimimela* to catch up. They allowed the horses to drink from the creek while they sat on the log that fell years ago.

"It's really beautiful here." She commented.

"Yes. I often come here when I need to think." He replied. "I feel at home here."

"So, there's no chance you'll remain on the reservation with us?" She asked hopefully.

"No. My home is here now. I will stay for my sister and her family." He said shaking his head.

"You could stay with me." She reached and took his hand.

"I'm sorry, but my heart belongs to someone else." He removed his hand as he stood. "We should get back."

When he helped her up, she surprised him with a lip-
lock that would have tempted most men. It took only
seconds before he knew for sure she wasn't the one he
loved. Elysa owned his heart and until he had
confirmation she didn't have feelings toward him, he
wouldn't betray his own feelings.

"*Kimimela*, I don't feel that way about you. I grew
up with you as a friend, I can't do that to our
friendship." He stepped away from her.

"It's that Elysa, isn't it?" *Kimimela* complained.

"Yes, it is. I knew the moment I met her she would
be my wife." He tried to keep from hurting her feelings.

"It's just as well. I knew you'd never return to our
village when you left." She said stepping away from
him. "I want to go now."

Shadow watched her leap onto Snowball's back and
gallop away. He watched her hair flying as she faded
into the distance. Reluctantly, he jumped on Cannon
Ball's back and trotted after her. The next few days
would be uncomfortable for them, but he hadn't
initiated that kiss, she had.

Chapter Thirty-three

The fall rodeo and festival just happened to fall on the weekend before Shadow started work. Saturday, Shadow, Star, Kevin, *Kimimela*, and *Enapay* dressed in their traditional clothing to entertain the crowd with their trick riding and dance, just after the mutton busting event for the little guys and gals.

Elysa sat with Samantha, Ginger, Jillian, and Kimberly in the stands to help with the little ones while Spencer rode his horse Buster in a roping contest. Then he and Will would watch over Dev as he rode in the mutton busting contest. When Dev won the crowd around Elysa jumped to their feet and cheered.

The music changed as The Lakota rode in with their authentic colorful costumes and painted horses. Everyone enjoyed the difficult tricks they performed before they leapt from their horses, grabbed their drums, and began their dance.

Elysa's eyes fell on the man she loved. He looked so handsome, yet wild with his long hair. At one point he looked up and met her eyes. Butterflies took wing in her stomach as she watched the show end.

Trace rode out on Nutmeg who had made him a lot of money. His careful breeding of him and Cinnamon brought people from all over the country looking to breed their horses with Nutmeg. One of the offspring won the Wyoming Downs championship.

The barrel racers followed behind him as the workers set up the barrels for the next event. Though Elysa watched, her mind remained on the Lakota man who'd stolen her heart.

"Is anyone thirsty?" She asked.

"Nope, but you can bring me a funnel cake with extra powdered sugar please." Jillian asked.

"Are you pregnant?" Ginger grinned, noting the glow on her face.

"Yes, but don't say anything. I'm telling Josh tonight." She beamed.

"Wow! I'd love to be a fly on the wall when you tell him." Ginger laughed.

"I'll be back shortly." Elysa slowly walked down the steps of the bleachers.

She decided to stop by the pen where she knew Shadow and his friends were grooming their horses. Star, *Enapay*, and his parents met her as she rounded the corner of the restroom. "Hi, Elysa, he's grooming his horse and loading all the horses up for transport home."

"Thanks, I really enjoyed your performance." Elysa smiled as she passed them.

Shadow listened to *Kimimela* talk of things that would never be. She knew he wasn't interested, but she wouldn't give up so easily.

When she spotted Elysa walking past Star and her family, she turned to Shadow again. "You know we can live in your father's old home. I will make it a home for us and our children. When we return to the reservation, Elder Dakota would be happy to marry us." *Kimimela* said cheerfully before purposely tripping and ending up in his arms.

Elysa heard every word as she neared the end of the trailer. When she saw Shadow holding her in his arms, she left to get Jillian's funnel cake. By the time she got back to her seat, Shadow and *Kimimela* had sat down next to Star.

Elysa gave Jillian her sweet treat and sat next to Samantha. She needed to be as far away from him as she could get. To her relief, Jarod showed up and sat next to her. He'd lost the calf roping competition to Will.

"I'm sorry Will beat you." She smiled sadly when he sat down.

"There's always next year." Jarod shrugged. "Do you wanna go to the bar when this is over?"

"I would thank you. I'm getting a little claustrophobic staying inside so much." She smiled happily even though Jarod wasn't her first choice for a date.

The rest of the afternoon seemed to go on forever. Seeing *Kimimela* fawn all over Shadow. He seemed to enjoy the attention. Finally, the rodeo ended, and she helped Ginger pack her brood into the SUV. Thankfully, the little ones gave up and fell asleep.

Chapter Thirty-four

Jarod helped her into his truck and drove into town. He led her inside to his favorite table next to the band. The cheery atmosphere did wonders for her heart. Well, until Shadow and *Kimimela* showed up.

"You all right?" Jarod asked when he saw the direction she focused on.

"Yes. Wanna dance?" She asked after taking a long pull on the beer she had.

Jarod expertly led her across the dance floor in a flawless two-step.

Before long Elysa was more than a little drunk. Jarod finally refused to let her have any more alcohol. It didn't matter to her; she was only drowning her sorrow. The minute she saw Shadow and *Kimimela* dancing the green-eyed monster came out in all its glory.

"Let's dance again." She slurred.

"I don't think that's a good idea, you can barely stay in that chair. Let me take you home." Jarod stood to help her up.

"I wanna dance!" She shouted.

"Okay, just calm down." Jarod took her hand.

On the dance floor, they passed Shadow who clearly wasn't a happy man. He got closer so he could switch partners with Jarod. The second she saw him, she laid a long lip-lock on Jarod, then shot Shadow a smirk.

"Take that you jerk." She thought angrily.

Shadow's face turned to granite as his jaw twitched. He led *Kimimela* to the door, and they left.

Jarod grabbed her upper arm and jerked her closer. "Are you trying to get me scalped?"

"He ain't gonna do nothin to you." She told him as a tear trickled from the corner of her eye. "He's got Hawk's sister to keep him company."

"I hope you're right. He didn't seem too happy to me." Jarod looked back at the closed door. "Let's get you home. Ginger and Frank are gonna be mad at me for letting you drink so much."

"They aren't my parents Jarod." Her speech slurred even more.

By the time Jarod pulled into Ginger's driveway, Elysa was snoring slightly. He sighed heavily when the front door opened, and Ginger stepped outside. Reluctantly he went around the truck and picked Elysa up then carried her inside to her room.

Frank and Ginger both sat at the dining table waiting for him. Unable to avoid the coming conversation, he sat down across from them.

"What happened tonight?" Ginger glared at him.

Jarod explained the entire evening. "I didn't instigate anything. Elysa drank too much and well you obviously know the rest."

"Star called and told us Shadow is on the warpath. I think you need to get away for a few days until he calms down." Ginger said.

"I was thinking the same thing. I don't want him scalping me in my sleep." Jarod sighed.

"He's leaving tomorrow to take Hawk's family home so I wouldn't worry about it too much." Frank grinned. "Shadow won't scalp you; he might make your life miserable for a few days, but he won't harm you." Ginger laughed.

"I honestly tried to get Elysa to stop drinking, but every time she saw Shadow and that lady, she'd order another drink and down it." Jarod said.

"She is an adult so I can't say anything. I'm sure she wouldn't take no for an answer." Frank grumbled.

"I'll see y'all later. I'm headed home." Jarod hugged Ginger and left.

"From what Star told me Shadow is really angry."
Ginger said. "He must love her to react like that."

"He does, and I'm sure Hawk's sister didn't make
things easy for her." Frank stood and helped her to her
feet. "Let's go to bed. The kiddo's will be up early."

Frank turned the lights out and locked everything up
tight. On his way upstairs he grinned thinking about
Jared's claim that Shadow would scalp him in his sleep.
After seeing the Lakota dance and trick riding, he could
actually envision that happening.

Ginger was already asleep when he slipped into the
bed with her. As always, she managed to get her cold
feet on his legs. He really needed to get her some
heated hunting socks to keep them warm.

Soon he was sound asleep for the first time in years
he felt at peace. Now that Durango was no longer a
threat he relaxed. The fact that Hawk was no longer
with them bothered him, but at his age he knew that no
one could hide from death when it knocked on the door.

Hawk went out as a hero by saving Shadow. Yes, he
still mourned his friend's loss but now he needed to
move on to raise his family. Lately he focused on
turning CFS over to Gordan. His role in the company
would be minimal from now on. He didn't want to miss
anything while his children grew.

Chapter Thirty-five

Shadow parked next to the small shack the Hawk family lived in. He offered them anything they wanted from his childhood home. Since his sister lived in Wolf Creek and his parents were gone, he saw no reason to hang onto what he left behind.

Kimimela took one last shot at marrying him even though she knew he wouldn't relent.

"That girl obviously doesn't want you. With the exception of Star, you have nothing to go back for." *Kimimela* insisted. "Stay here and let me be your wife."

"I don't feel that way about you, little Butterfly. My heart belongs to Elysa whether she marries me or not. There will be no other women in my life." Shadow replied sternly. "Goodbye."

He backed onto the dirt road and left her standing on the porch watching as he left. Hawk was the last tie binding him to the reservation. He would never return.

An hour after dark, the town of Widow's Bend appeared on the horizon as he slowed to the speed limit. The memory of finding out what Falcon and his friends had done to the sheriff and the owner of the diner flooded his mind.

Thank God Kevin had found them when he did. The final tragedy came when the diner owner wound up committing suicide unable to recover from the mental anguish the man created from torturing her.

Archer had intentions of asking her to marry him, but after her death, something broke in him. Joe talked him into leaving Widow's Bend after he retired. Now he happily provided security at the Silver Spur Ranch, Josh and his wife owned.

If only his life weren't so hard. Scarlet Bird had been the love of his life until she died. It took a long time to get over her and the loss of their child. At first his heart ached in a way he could've never imagined. Then when his mother succumbed to cancer, he couldn't take another loss in his life.

Now he couldn't help but love Elysa. When she entered a room, her energy brightened even the darkest of days. A snort escaped when he remembered her pink hair. She had recently went back to the color God gave her.

Within ten miles of Wolf Creek, he had just come around a curve and met the headlights of another car swerving into his lane. Jerking the steering wheel to the right to miss the person, his right front tire slipped off the shoulder and blew out. Desperately trying to keep from hitting the car still headed straight for him, he tried to keep the truck from flipping. The back right tire blew and sent his truck flipping over twice into a small gulley.

After the truck came to a stop on its side, and the air bag deployed he saw stars. At that moment, he wished he'd worn his seat belt properly. He had a habit of putting the shoulder strap behind him. Although the lower strap held him in the seat, during the tumble down the gulley, he broke his left arm and leg.

Darkness filled his vision as he tried to make sense of what happened. The split second before he lost consciousness he knew he couldn't stay where he was. No one would see him or his truck from the road.

Of course, the driver didn't get out to see if Shadow had any injuries let alone survived the collision. The sound of wheels spinning told him the truck left the scene, then nothing.

Several hours later, Shadow slowly opened his eyes to moonlight streaming through the broken windshield. When his mind cleared somewhat, he remembered thinking no one would see him from the road. He tried to find his cell phone, but gave up when he couldn't find it, not that he would have any service here.

Carefully moving his arms and legs he discovered his right side hadn't suffered serious injuries. Since he landed on its side, it appeared the only way to escape was through the broken windshield.

He managed to drag himself from the wreckage and halfway up the side of the gulley when the pain grew unbearable. Stopping to rest, the darkness he tried to keep at bay overtook him and he slid back down to the bottom of the gulley.

The sound of a wolf howling jolted Shadow out of his unconscious state. His eyes opened in the direction of the sound that normally wouldn't have caused him any concern, struck fear like he'd never felt before.

"Get up *Ohanzee*!" He heard Hawk's voice from behind him.

"Hawk?" He questioned his sanity.

"Yeah it's me. I leave you for a few days and you find yourself in trouble. Now get up and climb that hill!" Hawk's voice ordered.

"I can't, my arm and leg are broken." He sighed.

"The other arm and leg are fine. If you don't move, you're gonna be lunch for that pack of wolves." Hawk insisted. "Elysa is waiting for you, now are you gonna give up or go to her?"

"She's with Jarod." He growled.

"No, she's not. She heard *Kimimela* talking about marrying you and saw her fall into your arms at the rodeo. Jarod offered to take her out as a friend." Hawk told him.

"I saw her kiss him!" He bellowed as he pulled himself a foot up the hill.

"You know she had too much to drink. I'll wager she didn't know what she did." Hawk said.

Shadow pulled himself inch by inch up the side of the gulley until he finally reached the shoulder of the road. The sky to the east brightened as dawn came.

"I knew you could do it." Hawk said. "Now lay there on the grass and rest. Someone will come along and see you."

"You're leaving again aren't you?" He asked as the light dimmed into inky blackness.

He hoped someone would find him as he fell into nothingness.

Chapter Thirty-six

Elysa squinted against the fingers of light slowly crawling across the room. A moment of confusion washed over her as she opened her bloodshot eyes.

"Oh, my Lord what did I do last night?" She moaned.

"You got stupid drunk." Ginger said opening her door with a knock.

"Why didn't someone stop me?" She moaned holding her head.

"Jarod tried, but you wouldn't listen." Ginger held out a small mug of the foulest thing Elysa had ever smelled in front of her.

"I don't want that stuff, it's awful." She turned her nose up at it.

"Drink it and eat that toast. You know the drill." Ginger insisted.

As she downed the brew and ate the toast, she asked how she got home.

"Jarod brought you home after the incident at the bar." Ginger said. "You owe Shadow an apology."

Elysa choked on the bite of toast she tried to swallow. "Why?"

"You laid a hot and heavy lip-lock on Jarod when Shadow and Hawks sister were dancing." Ginger explained. "Jarod is terrified Shadow is gonna scalp him in his sleep."

"Shadow won't do that. It's a stupid joke and not very funny." Elysa grumbled. "Besides, I heard *Kimimela* and Shadow making wedding plans. I'm not gonna be that woman."

"Are you sure that's what you heard?" Ginger asked giving Elysa her full attention.

"Kinda hard not to hear it when they were talking about it while putting their horses on the trailer.

Besides, when I looked around the trailer, she was in his arms. It wasn't hard to figure out what was going on." She sniffed.

"You should talk to him about it. I'll bet you misread the situation." Ginger said.

"Whatever. I hope he's happy with that woman." She dabbed her eyes.

"Get cleaned up and we'll go to Sheridan and buy you a pretty dress that will make Shadow sit up and take notice."

"All right, but Shadow's taken, but it would be nice to find a pretty outfit." She perked up.

"I think you're wrong, but it's your life." Ginger shrugged. "Hurry up so we can get going."

Elysa jumped into the shower then quickly dressed for the day. By the time she got downstairs, Ginger had the kids ready to go.

They secured them in the car seats and were on their way. The trip to Sheridan was just what the doctor ordered. Elysa found some cute sundresses and sandals to match them.

After a burger and fries, they took the little ones to the park so they could run off some energy.

"Thank you Ginger for insisting we do this today. I needed to get away from town for a few hours." Elysa said gratefully.

"To be honest so did I." She said keeping a close eye on her toddlers. "Don't get me wrong, I love your brother and the home we built together, but I just need to get away once in a while."

Elysa sat quietly for a few moments, then asked, "Do you really think I'm wrong about Shadow?"

"Yes, I do. Shadow doesn't step into anything without giving it a lot of thought first. I'm sure he hadn't had any contact with Hawk's family since he left the reservation over ten years ago." Ginger replied.

"So, I should give him a chance to explain?" She asked guessing what Ginger was thinking.

"I think he'll want you to explain what happened last night. From what Jarod said, he was furious enough to leave the bar." Ginger said.

"I messed things up bad didn't I?" She hung her head.

"It's nothing that you can't fix. Sometimes the choices we make have consequences we have to reconcile before we can move on." Ginger responded.

"Like you and Frankie?" She said sniffing back tears.

"Yes. I nearly lost him because of my stupid stubbornness. If Joe hadn't arrested me, I don't think we would have moved forward in our relationship. I was so cruel to him, I'm still in awe that he stepped in to help me." Ginger wiped away a tear and stood. "We should get the kiddo's back. They'll need baths before dinner after playing in the sand pile."

Soon they were back on the road to Wolf Creek. Elysa thought long and hard about her situation. Did she want to deal with the angry Lakota man? Would he forgive her for being stupid? More importantly, did she love him enough to spend her life with him?

Elysa didn't realize they had arrived home until Ginger parked the SUV. "Wow, I didn't realize we were home already."

"You were doing some heavy thinking. I left you alone." Ginger opened her door. "Let's get these little angels inside."

In no time, Ginger had all for babies fed and bathed. With Elysa's help the little tykes were sound asleep.

"Have you made a decision on what to do about Shadow?" Ginger asked.

"I'll have to apologize. That means I'll have to listen to his side of the story with that woman." Elysa sagged into the chair.

"You never know how much it will affect your future with someone just by listening. That was my biggest problem with your brother. I wouldn't listen to anyone. It was obvious to everyone but me that Frank loved me. That's what almost cost me my future." Ginger replied.

"I understand. I'll talk to him when I see him again." Elysa relented.

Chapter Thirty-seven

Shadow became aware of sirens blaring in the distance. How long had he laid there unconscious? He opened his eyes to see a sheriff he didn't know.

"Easy, you've got some serious injuries going on. The paramedics are almost here to help you." The man put a hand on his shoulder.

"What time is it?" He asked confused.

"Eleven a.m. You're dang lucky I had business in Wolf Creek this morning or no one would've seen you laying here." The sheriff of Widow's Bend answered as the ambulance parked on the shoulder of the road.

The paramedics finally put him in the back of the ambulance then transported him to the Wolf Creek hospital. The sheriff followed them in and stopped to see Josh before going to take Shadow's statement.

"Hey, Wally." Jarod waved him into his office. "What brings you to town?"

"I have some information on that home invasion out our way. I though you would like to have what I've gathered just in case they hit any ranches out this way." Wally said. "Good thing I did too. Some guy rolled his truck about ten miles from here. They took him to your new hospital. I'm heading over there to get his statement." Wally told him.

"Oh? Do you know who he was?" Josh's radar went off.

"Some guy. His truck is at the bottom of that gully just before the curve ten miles from here. He looked Native American. I still don't know how he dragged himself to the top of the gulley. He has some serious injuries." Wally said.

"I'm coming with you. I think I know who it is." Josh jumped to his feet.

Wally followed Josh as he hurried from the police station toward the hospital.

"This guy must be important for you to rush over there." Wally commented.

"He's the man who taught me to fight." Josh said pushing the ER doors open.

"I've seen you fight, if he taught you he's gotta be formidable." Wally said surprised.

"He saved my brother's life after a full-grown grizzly attacked him." Josh said as he stopped at the nurse's station.

"They have him in surgery. He has some internal injuries they need to repair. I was just about to call Star." The nurse informed him.

"I'll take care of that. We'll be in the waiting room when they finish patching him up." Josh took out his cell phone.

Soon Star ran in with Trace following close behind.

***

Elysa jumped when Ginger's cell phone chirped beside her.

"Hello?" Ginger answered.

"Is Elysa still there?" Frank asked.

"Yes, why?" She asked.

"Just don't let her leave, I'm on my way to pick her up. Call Sandy and ask her to come watch the kids." He said. "I'll be there soon."

"What's going on?" She wanted answers.

"Just do what I ask Red. I'll be there to explain in a few minutes." Frank insisted.

"Okay." She ended the call and dialed Dillon's number.

"Hello?" Sandy's cheerful voice answered.

"Hey, Frank wants you to watch the kids. He didn't say why, but it sounds serious." Ginger explained.

"We'll be right over." Sandy said and ended the call.

"What's going on?" Elysa asked as Frank's truck parked in the drive.

"I don't know, Frank's here to tell us." Ginger said, going toward the door.

"Did you call Sandy?" He asked as he kissed her cheek.

"Yes, what's going on." Ginger asked.

"Come sit with Elysa." He led her to a chair.

"What's wrong Frankie?" Elysa asked as her stomach clenched.

"Shadow's been in an accident. He's…" He began.

"Let's go! I want to see him!" Elysa jumped to her feet.

"When Sandy gets here we'll go. He's in surgery so we don't know much." He promised.

Elysa practically flew out of the door when Sandy arrived with the younger Smalley children.

"We'll be back soon." Ginger hugged her and joined Elysa and Frank in his truck.

The minute she spotted Star when they walked into the waiting room, she hurried to her.

"What happened?" She asked breathlessly.

"All we know is he rolled his truck." Star sniffed.

"Have they told you anything?" She asked.

"Not yet." Trace answered for his wife. "You may as well sit and wait with the rest of us."

Two long anxious hours later, Doc Sims stepped into the room.

"He'll make it. we put temporary pins and rods in the leg until it heals and put a cast on his broken arm. The thing that concerns us is the concussion. We're monitoring him closely for swelling in the brain." Doc explained. "Did he fall asleep at the wheel?"

"We don't know yet. Sheriff Wally Johnson from Widow's Bend found him on the side of the road. His truck is at the bottom of the gulley. That's all he knows." Josh told him.

"At any rate, when they move him to his room, y'all can see him. Keep it down to no more than four at a time. He'll be groggy from the anesthetic." Doc said. "I'll see y'all around."

Star, Trace, Josh, and Sheriff Johnson were the first to see him. Although relieved he survived, they worried about the concussion. The bruises and cuts from the windshield on his face concerned them too. They talked quietly until Shadow opened his eyes. Disoriented, he tried to sit up, but Trace and Josh kept him from moving.

"It's all right Shadow, you're in the hospital." Star's voice registered.

Immediately he quit fighting with relief flooding him.

"Can you tell us what happened." Wally asked waiting patiently for an answer.

"Some *GNAYE,* fool, ran me off the road." He replied angrily. "They didn't even stop to see if I was okay."

"Can you give me a description of the vehicle?" Wally asked.

"No. The guy was in my lane with his bright lights on." He shook his head regretting it the moment he did.

"That's not much to go on, but I'll check out the scene and see what we come up with." Wally said turning to leave. "Is there any place we can tow your truck. I'm afraid it's a total loss."

"No, I'll call my insurance company so they can tow it." He said.

"Okay then. I'll let you know what I find after I look at the scene again." Wally said leaving the room.

"I guess this means you won't be starting work tomorrow does it?" Josh said.

"Clearly not. I don't suppose you can hold the job for me?" Shadow asked hopefully.

"I'm sure we'll survive until you're on your feet again." Josh said. "I'll see if Kevin wants to go with me to the scene of the accident. Wally's a good investigator but Kevin is better."

"I'd feel better if you did." He winced as the pain medication began wearing off.

"I'll go so someone else can visit you." Josh said before leaving.

Star gently hugged him as Trace stood behind her.

"We'll get you moved into the spare room so Star can nurse you back to health." Trace insisted.

"I don't want to be a burden." He winced again. "If you can care for me at my house during the day, I'll hire someone to help me in the evenings."

Trace and Star left shortly after giving him a moment to call the nurse for more pain meds.

Chapter Thirty-eight

Elysa followed Frank and Ginger to Shadow's room. She wondered if he would even want to see her after the stunt she pulled at the bar. At least he knew she had drank too much and hopefully would believe she didn't know what she was doing.

Frank knocked on the open door to draw Shadow's attention.

"Come on in." He said as his eyes fell on Elysa.

"Man, you sure got banged up didn't you?" Frank commented.

"Yeah, somebody ran me off the road. I'd be willing to bet they were driving drunk." He shifted the head of the bed a bit higher.

"I'm glad you survived. From what the Sheriff of Widow's Bend said, you're lucky to be alive." Frank said.

"Yeah, I know." He agreed.

"Who's going to take care of you after the Doc releases you?" Ginger asked.

"Star can take care of me in the daytime, but I'll have to hire someone to help the rest of the time." He replied.

"I can help after four p.m. I have a job from eleven to three." Elysa spoke up.

"What will your boyfriend say to that?" He asked angrily.

"Uh, Frank I think we should leave them to talk." Ginger grabbed his hand.

"Yeah sure. We'll be in the waiting room when you're done." Frank agreed.

The room filled with a heavy silence as Shadow's eyes bore into her. She felt so bad she couldn't meet his gaze.

"I'm sorry Shadow. Jarod isn't my boyfriend. He took me out because I was upset. Then ignoring his warnings, I drank too much. After I saw you with that Lakota woman dancing, I couldn't stop myself." She apologized. "Maybe you should have Kevin go pick her up so she can stay with you."

"Why would I do that?" He didn't understand.

"I heard y'all talking about getting married. Then I saw her in your arms and figured I was in the way of your relationship." She managed around the painful lump growing in her throat.

"I have no relationship with *Kimimela* other than friendship. I will never see her or Hawk's family again. There is nothing to hold me there any longer. After Hawk died, so did my ties to the reservation." He explained. "I'm sorry if I gave you the wrong impression."

"Can we start over?" She looked up with tears in her eyes.

"Yes." He reached for her hand. "Hi, I am *Ohanzee*."

"I'm Elysa, it's nice to meet you." She smiled wiping the tears from her cheeks.

They talked for several minutes when Will and Samantha knocked and entered the room.

"How are you feeling." Samantha asked with deep concern for him.

"I've survived worse than this. I'll be fine." He smiled at the woman who became the surrogate mother for everyone in Wolf Creek.

"I'm glad to hear it." Samantha relaxed.

"Tell us what happened." Will asked.

Shadow went through the entire story, leaving his conversation with Hawk out of it. "The sheriff of Widow's Bend found me, or I'd still be laying on the side of the road."

"I'll get some of the women in town to help care for you after you go home." Samantha said.

"No need. Star will take care of me while Elysa is at work." Shadow declined.

After a long visit everyone cleared out of his room and the nurses settled him in for the long night ahead.

Between the pain meds wearing off and the nurses waking him every two hours, he didn't get any rest. When morning came he was in the foulest of moods.

Doc Sims showed up and examined him again. "Looks like you're gonna be fine. I'll see about releasing you tomorrow. Are you gonna stay with Star and Trace?"

"No, Star will watch me in the day while Elysa is working. When she gets off work, she'll come stay with me." He replied.

"Good, I'll see you this afternoon. If you're still improving I'll let you go home tomorrow. I'm still concerned about your concussion." Doc said. "You're a lucky man from what I hear."

"I guess so." He simply responded.

"Uh oh. What's going on?" Doc pulled a chair up and sat down.

"Nothing really. I'm just frustrated. I had plans to ask Elysa out on a date then that maniac kidnapped her. I thought after we rescued her I'd have a chance, then Hawk sacrificed himself for my happiness with Elysa. I had to set her straight about Hawk's sister. I don't have feelings for the woman, but she threw herself at me and Elysa witnessed it. She thought I was engaged to her." Shadow sighed.

"Does she know you love her?" Doc grinned.

"Not yet. Now that I'm laid up, I won't be able to take her out on a date." He grumbled.

"Don't worry about it, things will work out." Doc said. "I gotta finish my rounds. See you this afternoon."

Shadow watched the old country doctor leave the room. Even though this was the first time he had to care for him, Doc proved to be an excellent physician.

With some difficulty he moved into a more comfortable position and fell asleep. Thankfully, the nurses left him alone so he could rest.

Chapter Thirty-nine

Elysa made mistake after mistake because she kept thinking about helping Shadow. Between excitement and nervousness, she found herself unable to focus on anything.

"What's going on Elysa?" Kelly asked. "You seem preoccupied today."

"I'm going to stay with Shadow after work. Doc released him this morning. Star and Trace took him home and she's staying with him until I can get there."

"Ah. Don't worry, you'll be fine. Shadow may act like a strong proud man, but he's no different from the other guys around these parts." Kelly tried to ease her worry.

"I know, it's just…" She took a deep breath. "I think I love him. I haven't even had a date with him, and I can't seem to quit thinking about him. When they told me he was in the hospital I nearly went out of my mind."

"I'm sure it will all work out." Kelly stood to give her the seat at the reception/dispatch desk. "I'm going to lunch. I'll see you in a half an hour."

Elysa sat down as Kelly left the building hoping nothing urgent would come up before she got back. Her thoughts returned to Shadow until the door opened and her heart immediately raced in fear.

Standing before the desk was a man who could pass for Marty Durango's twin.

"Excuse me, I'm looking for the sheriff." The man said.

"Um, sure. What is your name so I can give it to him." She squeaked.

"Charles Durango." The man's deep voice sent chills down her spine.

She picked up the phone and told Josh the man was there to see him as she tried to keep her voice steady. He told her to contact Frank and Will.

"He'll be right out." She told him dialing Frank's number.

"Thanks." Charles said and stood nearby waiting.

"Hello, I'm Josh, the sheriff of Wolf Creek. What can I do for you." Josh said with authority. "Come on back to my office."

Elysa watched them go down the hall as Frank answered his phone. She hurried to tell him what Josh said. Frank said he'd pick up Will and they'd be there shortly.

Inside the office, Josh studied the man who they though was dead. Marty had called him Paul when they had him cornered.

"You look as though you're seeing a ghost. Let me explain." The man began.

"If you wouldn't mind, I have someone coming that needs to hear what you have to say." Josh stopped him. "You look exactly like Marty, are you twins?" Josh asked as Frank and Will arrived.

The two men looked at the well-dressed man sitting patiently across from Josh trying to reconcile the fact he was identical to Marty Durango.

"Yes, actually. Jeffrey is my older brother by one minute, and Marty is two minutes younger than I am." Charles explained.

Frank and Will sat down staring at the man they believed was dead.

"So, you're the second of triplets?" Josh affirmed.

"Yes." Charles acknowledged.

"Now that Frank and Will are here, you may tell us your story.

"Surely. We were a surprise to our mother, of course we never knew who our father was, nor did we care once we grew up. Our mother worked three jobs to keep us fed and clothed. When we were old enough to leave, Marty joined the army. I worked and put myself through school and have a business degree. Our brother Jeffrey went into computer software design and is living in Silicon Valley." Charles explained. "Marty had issues after he was born due to having the umbilical cord wrapped around his neck, and he was blue when the doctor delivered him. The team worked until Marty took his first breath. We never suspected he had a mental problem growing up. He was good at hiding his feelings. After his stint in the brig, we lost track of him."

"So, you're saying he's had a mental problem all this time?" Will couldn't believe his ears. "How did he get through life without anyone knowing? Surely someone noticed."

"Marty may have had a mental problem, but he was smart and devious. None of us suspected how ill he was until we received a letter last month from him." Charles explained. "I've come to take him home and bury him."

"If you don't mind, I'd like to know what the letter said." Josh asked.

"Basically, he confessed to several murders for hire and a kidnapping. I suspect from the letter he had a split personality because parts of it seemed as though someone else wrote it. The handwriting and tone of the letter changed dramatically." Charles told them. "I followed the postmark here. I picked up the local newspaper and found the story written about what he'd done. I'm truly sorry he hurt anyone in this town."

"Thank you. We're just glad he's at rest now." Josh said.

"If there is anything I can do to compensate the town for my brother's outrage, let me know. Maybe I could donate to a special fund for the families lost in his rampage." Charles offered.

"That's a fine idea. Some of the families are suffering because of lack of funds due to Marty's assault on the town." Will said. "My wife told me Marty's other personality's name was Paul. Does that name mean anything to you?"

"Yes, he had a friend when he was younger named Paul. There was an accident, but no one could figure out how it happened. Marty was the only witness and he claimed he didn't remember." Charles explained. "He never spoke of his friend after that. Paul and I tried to help him, but he vehemently refused. Over the years, he grew to hate us because we wanted to make something of ourselves. Marty seemed to gravitate toward a violent career. Thus, he joined the army. We never understand how he fooled everyone so well. Now if you can point me in the direction of where my brother's body is, I'd like to settle things. Let me know a good amount to settle the destruction my brother caused your town and I'll write a check for it."

"How do you put a price on the lives lost, let alone the destruction of property?" Frank asked angrily.

"I suppose you can't, but trust me, I have the money to make restitution for his actions. Name your price." Charles sounded apologetic.

After he wrote a generous check, Josh showed him to the morgue.

Chapter Forty

Shadow grew anxious watching the clock. In two hours, Elysa would arrive to take over his care from Star. He shifted on the couch to a more comfortable position.

The cast on his leg went from his toes to the middle of his thigh. The cast bent at the knee so he couldn't straighten it out. Doc made him promise to keep the leg elevated for the first few days, then he could sit in the wheelchair the Wolf brothers kept on hand. It made it difficult to take care of his personal needs, but he made sure Star knew he didn't need her help at those times. His only worry was Elysa and her stubborn streak. Would she ignore him and try to help anyway? Not if he could help it she wouldn't.

"Are you ready for your pain meds?" Star asked putting little Allen in the playpen for a nap.

"If I have to." He grumbled. His sister knew how to care for him since she finally passed her RN tests. Doc Sims had nothing but praise for her dedication and conscientiousness.

"*Ohanzee*, I can't make you do anything. If you don't want them that's fine, however when the pain gets unbearable, you'll have to wait for them to take effect. It's best to stay ahead of it for now. In a few days, we'll cut back like Doc Sims ordered." She said leaving to get him a drink and the medicine.

When she returned he reluctantly took the pills and washed them down with the water she handed him.

"Who's a good boy?" She laughed.

"It ain't funny *Winchapi!*" He barked.

"I'll leave you to nap, is there anything else I can help you with?" She said schooling her face. Shadow was a proud man; he wouldn't take her pity or sympathy well.

"No." He said as she fluffed the pillow under his leg.

"I'll be cleaning the room off the kitchen for you. If you need anything…" She moved toward the door.

"I won't." He grumbled wishing he could turn onto his side.

***

Elysa looked at the clock for what seemed a millionth time to find the second hand had only moved five minutes. She still had an hour to go before she could leave. With a heavy sigh, she continued filing the paper copies of the reports Josh and the deputies generated the day before.

When she saw the stack of papers on her desk, she couldn't believe how many crazy things people called the sheriff's office for.

Some of them she understood, like when the older folks couldn't manage certain situations by themselves. Others she thought were a waste of the deputy's time.

James stepped out of his office and asked if she was ready to photograph a crime scene.

Without a word she grabbed her camera and followed him outside to his official Jeep.

"Where are we off to?" She asked buckling herself in.

"Someone left a body in the field at the Anderson Ranch. Deputy Combs found it when he stopped to check on things. I hope you have a strong stomach; he said the body was severely decomposed." James said.

"I'll have to since it's my job to photograph everything." She swallowed. It wasn't something she thought about when she accepted the position.

The ride was silent as she worked to conquer the butterflies fluttering in her stomach. When James parked the Jeep, she took a deep breath and stepped from the vehicle. With her camera hanging from around her neck, she grabbed the kit James and Josh helped her put together.

Deputy Warren Combs got out of his truck and led them to the pasture past the barn while giving James the details of what he'd found.

Elysa's stomach lurched when the smell hit her from fifty feet away. Her face paled as she worked to keep from gagging.

"Are you alright?" James asked.

Unable to speak, she nodded her head and reluctantly followed the men. She watched them pull handkerchiefs out and cover their noses and mouths wondering how she could hold a handkerchief and take pictures of the deceased person.

"Looks like a man, but we'll have to wait for the coroner's report to figure out how he died." Warren said.

"Someone shot him at close range." James told him kneeling down to out faint powder burns on the man's shirt. "Elysa, get a picture of this, then start photographing the body."

Elysa obeyed and managed to get all the pictures James wanted before running back to the barn and losing her lunch.

"Are you okay?" James asked when she turned to rejoin the men.

"Yeah. Are we finished?" She asked wiping her eyes and mouth.

"Yes. When we get back to the office, get the pictures off your camera and send them to me." James said leading her back to the Jeep.

He stopped to speak with the new coroner, Willis Conners. After the conversation, he left Warren and the coroner to move the body.

Elysa closed her eyes to ward off the nausea still lingering.

James remained silent. He had to give her credit; she got all the pictures he needed before getting sick. He remembered the first time he had to deal with a decaying body. She managed to keep it together longer than he had.

"We're here, get those to me asap." James said parking in front of the station.

"You'll have them in a few minutes." She hopped out of the Jeep and went inside.

True to her word, she composed an email and sent the pictures to James before leaving for the day.

Chapter Forty-one

Shadow looked up when Elysa stepped into the house with her suitcase in hand. There was no mistaking the green pallor of her face.

"What's wrong?" He scooted up on the couch.

"I had my first experience of a decayed body. I worked through it, but Eww!" She grimaced.

Shadow quickly bit back the smile forming on his face. He too had the unfortunate experience as a young tribal law enforcement officer.

Star came around the corner to greet her and pick up baby Allen. "Did you have a long day?"

"Yes. I'll be alright after a shower." She replied. "Which room do you want me in?"

"Take your pick. I borrowed Samantha's baby monitor to put by your bed so if *Ohanzee* needs you during the night you can hear him." Star grinned.

"I ain't no baby." Shadow growled from the couch."

"You are until you can get around by yourself, so deal with it my brother." Star laughed.

"Will you be okay while I change?" Elysa asked.

"Yes. Take your time." Shadow insisted.

Star left as Elysa hurried upstairs to shower. Somehow she had to get the stench from that body out of her nose. After the hot shower, she felt much better and could breathe easier. She went back downstairs to see what Shadow wanted for dinner.

"Are you hungry?" She asked when his attention fell on her.

"I could eat. Just fix whatever you want." He said watching her closely.

"Okay, I'll be right back. Do you need anything before I start cooking?" She hesitated before turning to leave.

"Nope, I'll just lay here and be a good boy." He muttered.

He missed the smile that formed on Elysa's lips as she hurried into the kitchen to see what was in the pantry. Her mother taught her how to cook before she became too sick to prepare their meals.

The smells coming from the kitchen drifted into the den teasing Shadow's nose. His stomach immediately began growling. It was an uncomfortable feeling being that hungry. In his mind that was an added discomfort he didn't need. Never in his life had he been in this condition, and it made him angry.

Frustrated, he grabbed the wheelchair by the armrest and pulled it closer to the couch. He locked the side closest to him but couldn't reach the other side. Lifting his leg off the pillows, he sat up. Still unable to reach the wheel lock on the other side, he held onto the armrest and tried to stand and twist himself into the seat of the chair. Just as he turned the unlocked wheel moved and he fell with a loud thud.

Elysa heard him hit the floor and came running. The sight of Shadow struggling to sit up sent her heart into overdrive. "What do you think you're doing?"

"What does it look like?" He growled. "Help me up!"

Quickly rushing to his side, she managed to help him back onto the couch with a great deal of difficulty. Elysa was so small, and Shadow was tall and lanky. Add in the cast on his arm and the one on his leg, he was quite heavy.

"There." She sighed fluffing the pillow under his foot. "Now would you mind telling me why you were on the floor?"

"I wanted to go into the dining room. Whatever you're cooking is driving me crazy with hunger." He explained as his stomach growled.

"You couldn't wait five minutes for me to help you?" She put her fisted hands on her hips. "You silly man, don't you know you could've done more damage to yourself? What if something shifted when you fell?"

"You ain't no doctor so don't tell me what could've happened." He glared at her. "Besides, I can take care of myself."

"Clearly. You know if you don't need any help, I can go back home." She snorted.

"No! I mean... I'm sorry but I'm not used to having to depend on someone else for everything." He quickly explained.

"Look. I understand, but you have to let your body heal or you could wind up a cripple. If that happens you'll have to depend on others the rest of your life." She told him. "I'm here for you now, so if you wanna come to the dining room, I'll help you into your chair."

"Okay." He relented.

After a short struggle he rested his leg on the footrest of the chair as she pushed him into the dining room. When he was situated at the table, she brought him a plate of food.

"That smells fantastic." He inhaled the enticing scent.

"Thanks. Now eat up, there's plenty for seconds if you wish." She replied and sat down to eat her plate of food.

"So, are you enjoying your job?" He asked.

"Up until this afternoon I've loved every minute of it." She grimaced and pushed her plate away losing her appetite.

"It's rough dealing with a dead body, especially if it's decomposing." Shadow said.

"I just hope that isn't a regular thing. I'll still do my job, but that will be the part I hate." She sighed.

"Do they have any clues to who did it or what happened?" He asked.

"Not as far as I can tell. I just wanted out of there. They can figure out the who done it." She shook her head. "I suppose tomorrow James is going to show me how to read the evidence."

"I always did like the forensic part of the investigation." He told her. "At one point I wanted to be a forensic scientist, but it takes too long to get a degree and I didn't have the money."

"What about now?" She asked.

"I suppose I could enroll in a few courses while I'm laid up." He replied thoughtfully. "Star studied online; I suppose I could too."

"You should talk to Josh. Maybe the department will help you like they did Star. She had to agree to work so many years for their help. I think it's a great option if Josh will go for it." She suggested.

"I'll call him later. Thanks for suggesting that." He smiled at her.

Elysa couldn't help the butterflies that took flight in her stomach when he smiled. His hard lined features softened into the most handsome man she'd ever seen. Even when she lived in New York photographing male models. None of them can compare to Shadow.

"Elysa?" He asked.

"Oh. Uh… What's wrong?" She jumped.

"I'd like to go to my room now." He said. "Where'd you go?"

"I was just wool gathering." She grabbed the handles on his wheel chair and backed him away from the table. After pushing him to the bedroom off the kitchen, she locked the wheels in the bathroom and left him to take care of his business while she fixed a tub of warm water and put it on the rolling table with soap and a washcloth.

"I'm through!" He called from the bathroom.

After settling him into the hospital bed, she pushed the table next to him.

"Just what are you planning to do with that?" He glared at her.

"I'm giving you a sponge bath. Don't take this wrong but you stink." Her tone left no room for argument. "Don't worry, You can wash your uh…"

He bit back a grin when her face flamed. "Chicken?"

"Oh stop!" She grabbed the soapy cloth and washed his arm, feet, and legs. Then made him sit up so she could wash his back. "There, now here's the washcloth. When you're done just holler and I'll take all this away."

After he finished, true to her words, she removed everything, and gave him his medicine.

"Would you tuck me in and read me a story?" He grinned at her.

"What are you, five?" She asked sarcastically.

"I figured if you were being so accommodating I'd ask." He laughed.

"Go to sleep Shadow." She said turning the baby monitor on. "If you need anything, just holler I'll hear you. Goodnight."

"Goodnight Elysa." He said wishing he could keep her there for the company.

The door closed behind her, and she let out a frustrated breath. Lordy how was she gonna take care of him and not keep her feelings hidden. When he looked at her with such longing in his eyes it was all she could do to keep from touching him.

Chapter Forty-two

The day finally came when Shadow was free from his cast on his arm and leg. Then he started therapy to gain strength back in his leg and arm. During the weeks of letting Elysa care for him, he knew he couldn't live without her. He'd already asked Frank for her hand to which Frank said. "It's about time."

Star drove him to Sheridan one afternoon to help him pick out a ring for Elysa.

"Are you sure about this?" She asked as she parked the minivan Trace had given her for her birthday.

"Yes. Don't get me wrong, I still love Scarlet Bird, but I've moved on. The love I have for Elysa far outshines the love I had for Scarlet Bird." He assured her.

The choices in the jewelry store intimidated him a little bit. Star helped him pick a gold ring with two hearts linked with a diamond in the center. The clerk happily made the sale wishing him good luck.

Star stopped at the diner in Wolf Creek after their little trip and they talked about when and where he would propose to her.

"I don't want anyone else around when I ask her. If she says no, I don't need to see pity in everyone's eyes." He told her.

"That's a wise decision." She agreed. "You should do it soon since you're getting around better now."

"I will. Here's what I need you to do." He agreed.

Elysa dreaded going back to Shadow's house knowing any day now he'd tell her he didn't need her any longer. She was going to miss sitting on the deck at night watching the stars and talking with him.

He told her about growing up on the reservation and all the adventures he had with Hawk and Kevin. She cried when he told her about Scarlet Bird and how she died. When he talked of his mother's illness and death her heart broke for him and Star.

She told him how much her father loved her mother and how he lost his leg in the war. The fun she had growing up with Frank and how she felt when he joined the military. Her sorrow over her mother passing and then losing her father.

She regaled him with stories of her time in New York and photographing the models for the magazines.

Her stomach hurt to think she wouldn't see him as much.

"Elysa, can I have the file on the body you pictured at the Anderson ranch?" James asked.

"Sure." She walked to the filing cabinet and pulled the file. "Here you go."

James opened it and picked two pictures out to study. His scrutiny made her nervous.

"Is there anything wrong?" She asked.

"What do you see here?" He handed the two photos over for her to look at.

Elysa studied the images closely. At the time there wasn't a reason to snap those particular photos, she wanted to make sure everything was in focus. Looking at both pictures she saw the same object on the ground barely sticking out of the dirt.

"What do you see?" He asked.

"Something sticking out of the dirt. What is it?" She squinted to see more clearly.

"I don't know, wanna go check it out?" He grinned.

"Is the odor from that body gone?" She looked up as the color drained from her face.

"After this long and the amount of rain we had last week, I'm sure you won't smell anything." He replied.

"Let's go." She grabbed her camera and the kit they had assembled for her.

James parked by the barn at the Anderson ranch fifteen minutes later. They made their way to the area where James found the body careful to examine the ground they walked on.

"Is this the area you took the picture in?" James asked studying the ground.

"Yes." She replied kneeling down to brush the grass and loose dirt away. "Look!"

James used his gloves, picked up a shell, and examined it. "Looks like a nine-millimeter. The coroner said the gunshot wound was a through and through. That means we have to find the bullet."

Elysa looked at him with bewilderment. "How are we gonna find a bullet in this pasture?"

"Easy, I have a metal detector in my Jeep." He chuckled.

Thirty minutes later they found what they were looking for. "Let's get this over to the lab at the hospital and see what they say." James put it in a small baggy.

When they returned to the station James had an idea who had shot the unidentified man.

Elysa wanted to know who they arrested, but after a visit with Joe, it turned out they had to wait for the sheriff of Widow's Bend to return their call before they could move forward.

Unwilling to put off going to Shadow's any longer, she left for the day.

Chapter Forty-three

Shadow watched his sister set up the romantic dinner for him and Elysa. Although it went against his nature and the traditional upbringing he had, his sister knew how a woman felt.

"I hope you're right about this." He said still doubting her idea.

"I know I am. She's not from the Lakota, and I've learned many things from Ginger, Samantha, and Jillian. When she comes home, give her the flowers, and send her upstairs to clean up from work. When she comes downstairs light the candles and seat her like Will does Samantha.." Star instructed him. "Pour the wine Ginger sent over and enjoy the meal. Compliment her by telling her how nice she looks. Thank her for taking care of you all this time. Then have a casual conversation with her, you'll know when to ask her to marry you."

"Do you think she'll say yes?" He asked nervously.

"I'm going to take one of her phrases. You silly man, if you'd pay more attention, you'd know she loves you." Star bumped his shoulder. "Now, I'm gonna leave before she arrives. Good luck my brother."

For the first time ever, Shadow initiated the hug for his sister. She patted his back and said, "Don't worry, you've got this as Will would say."

Shadow watched her take little Allen and walk out the back door. He sat down and rehearsed what to say once again. It struck him as funny he wasn't this nervous when he asked Scarlet Bird to be his wife. It cost him a lot of money to gain her father's permission.

Elysa parked her little beamer next to Shadow's truck. Her heart was heavy knowing that soon he would tell her he didn't need her anymore. Why, oh, why did she have to fall in love with the silly man. But love him she did.

Reluctantly, she gathered her camera and purse, then opened the car door. Soon she was at the front door using the key Shadow had given her to go inside.

The first thing she noticed made her stomach growl. The decadent smells coming from the kitchen surprised her. Did he cook dinner for them?

The second thing she saw was Shadow, in a nice suit, standing with a big bouquet of roses for her.

"These are for you." He gave the flowers to her. "Go on upstairs and dress for dinner."

Speechless, she did as he asked wondering if all this was to soften the blow of basically giving her a pink slip.

After a short shower, she slipped into the sexiest dress she had thinking maybe he'll think twice about letting her go. Finally ready for battle, she went downstairs.

Shadow heard her door open and lit the candles. Then rehearsed the instructions Star had given him. His heart felt like it would jump from his chest it was beating so fast.

"Shadow? What's all this?" She stepped into the dining room.

"I want to thank you for taking such good care of me. Come have a seat." He held the chair out for her.

When she sat down he pushed the chair a bit too close to the table. Adjusting for it, Elysa wondered why he was so jumpy. She watched him struggle with the cork on the wine bottle until it finally popped and flew across the room.

Finding it hard not to laugh, she managed to cover her smile. Shadow poured the wine into the glasses Star had set out for him. Since he'd never drank wine he had no idea how much to put in the glasses, so he filled them to the brim.

Elysa carefully accepted the one he handed her without spilling it. He went into the kitchen to get the salads that Star had prepared. When they finished the salad he brought out the main course. Elysa graciously accepted the plate and watched him sit down with his own. So far he hadn't spilled or dropped anything, then he reached for the bread basket and knocked it over spilling wine all over the beautiful white lace table cloth.

From that point on nothing went right. When he moved to clean up the wine, he knocked over the candles and wax spilled over the edge of the cup beneath them.

Elysa jumped up to help and they knocked heads hard enough to see stars. Shadow grabbed his head and her arm to help her sit back down.

"This isn't what I had in mind when Star helped me put this together." He growled in frustration.

"You didn't have to go to all this trouble to tell me you don't need my help anymore." She sighed.

"That's not why I did this Elysa." He looked into her eyes.

"Then why?" She asked confused.

Swallowing he got on one knee and pulled the ring out of his pocket.

Elysa's eyes flew open and big fat tears filled them and fell down her cheeks.

"Will you become my wife?" He asked holding his breath in anticipation.

"You silly man!" She jumped into his arms. "Of course, I'll marry you!"

The kiss she rewarded him with told him all he needed to know. This stubborn, feisty little woman loved him.

"Let's finish eating before it gets cold." He untangled her arms from around his neck.

The rest of the evening went better than he could have ever imagined. Before they retired to their separate rooms, they made plans setting the date and inviting all their friends.

Chapter Forty-four

Elysa couldn't contain her excitement the day of her wedding. After three months of planning and organizing, everything fell into place.

Thanks to Artie Billings, they set the wedding up on a cliff at the back forty of his ranch, overlooking Wolf Creek.

Ginger, Samantha, Star and Jillian were standing up with her. Trace, Kevin, Will, and Josh would stand up with Shadow. Samantha and Star would help Amanda and Angela down the aisle as flower girls, while Will and Trace would help Frankie and Willie down the aisle as ring bearers.

Frank asked if he could enter the tent set up as a dressing room. The girls left them to talk.

Star took the opportunity to speak with her brother.

"Are you ready?" She asked noting how handsome he was in the black and white tux.

"Yes, even in this monkey suit I'm ready." He smiled at his sister.

"It's almost time. I just wanted to say I'm happy you found love again." She said hugging him.

"Thank you." He hugged her back.

She left him with this groomsmen and ring bearer's with happy tears in her eyes.

Frank looked at his baby sister wearing the expensive white wedding dress. Crystals reflected the light of the off the shoulder gown. Ginger fit the matching veil on her head.

"You look gorgeous." He smiled down at her. "Mom and Dad would've been so proud of you."

"Don't make me cry." She waved her hands in front of her face.

"It's about time to begin." Star said stepping into the tent.

A gentle cool breeze kissed the faces of everyone in attendance as Shadow took his place standing proud and tall watching the procession down the temporary long wooden walk way. When the stringed music changed he swallowed his nerves with his eyes glued on the tent she would exit.

Kevin nudged him from behind, "Breathe my brother."

Then she appeared. His mouth fell open unable to believe she could be any more beautiful than she already was. The minute her eyes connected with his, the world around them disappeared until Frank stood in front of them.

"If you hurt my sister, I'll kill you." Frank whispered as he placed her hand in Shadows.

Shadow acknowledged the promise and turned with Elysa to the preacher.

The ceremony turned comical when Shadow forgot the words he wanted to say and decided to wing it.

"Elysa, I think I loved you from the moment I met you. Pink hair and all." He laughed nervously. "But under that feisty rebel exterior I found the soft sweet caring person who stole my heart. I promise to love you with all my heart forever and a day."

Elysa looked at him through her tears and said. "You silly man. I knew the moment we argued over the job I took that caused so much grief and trouble for everyone. That's when you stole my heart. I promise to love you with all my heart forever and a day."

Later at the reception during their first dance as husband and wife, Shadow knew he was the luckiest man on earth.

Elysa knew that God had brought them together and He had blessed their marriage.

***

After the happy couple drove off for their honeymoon, everyone helped clean up and left for their homes.

Will and Samantha settled on the deck of their home to watch the sun slip behind the mountains while their children chased lightening bugs around the back yard.

"We've come a long way haven't we?" Samantha asked with love shining in her eyes.

"Yes we have. No one could've guessed a joke gone wrong would've brought so many couples happiness. I'll have to thank Billy and Susan again the next time we see them." Will's lips covered hers with the same feeling of their first kiss.

The End

I hope you have enjoyed sharing the lives of the Wolf Creek family. Look for more entertaining books in the future.

I invite you to leave a review on Amazon.com and thank you in advance.

Books in Heroes of Wolf Creek Series:

Will's Heart
Ginger's Hope
Trace's Star
Josh's Dream
Elysa's Savior

Other books by R. J. Stevens:

Charlie's Park Bench

Follow R.J. Stevens:

On Amazon
https://www.amazon.com/author/rjstevens

On Facebook:

https://www.facebook.com/rjstevensauthor

Made in the USA
Coppell, TX
29 January 2024

28036333R00111